TWELFTH NIGHT

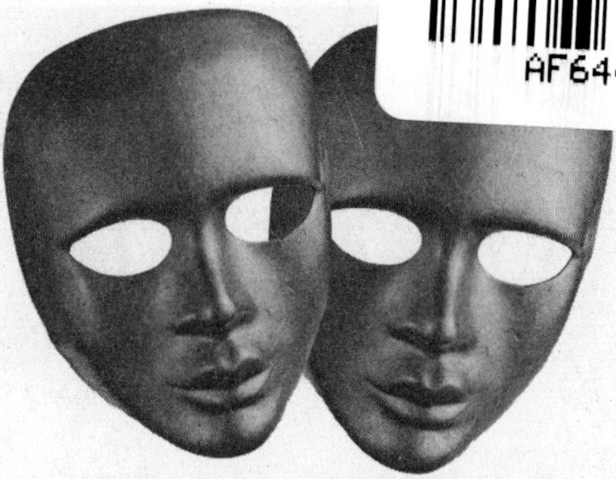

WILLIAM SHAKESPEARE

FP CLASSICS

Published 2025

FINGERPRINT! CLASSICS
Prakash Books

Fingerprint Publishing
@FingerprintP
@fingerprintpublishingbooks
www.fingerprintpublishing.com

ISBN: 978 81 7599 438 6

William Shakespeare began his career as an actor, writer, and part owner of a playing company called the Lord Chamberlain's Men, later known as King's Men, in London. Often regarded as the 'Bard of Avon' he is one of the world's pre-eminent dramatists. Born and brought up in Stratford-upon-Avon, he married Anne Hathaway at the age of eighteen and they had three children—Susanna, and twins Hamnet and Judith. Though few records survive of his private life, he appeared to have retired to Stratford around 1613 where he died three years later.

His works still in existence, including some collaborations, consist of thirty-eight plays, one hundred and fifty-four sonnets, two long narrative poems, and several other verses. His plays are performed much more than any other playwright's and have been translated in almost all major languages. Most of his known works have been produced between 1589 and 1613. His early plays were mainly comedies and histories which continue to be regarded as some of the best works produced in these genres.

Shakespeare's plays are difficult to date. His early classical and Italianate comedies contain tight double plots and precise comic sequences giving way to the romantic atmosphere of his most acclaimed comedies in the mid-1590s. *A Midsummer Night's Dream*—a witty mixture of romance, fairy magic, and comic low life scenes—is one of his most delightful creations shortly before he turned to *Romeo and Juliet. Romeo and Juliet* is his most famous romantic tragedy of sexually charged adolescence, love, and death. It marks a departure from his earlier works and from others of the English Renaissance.

His plays demonstrate the expansiveness of his imagination and the extent of his learning. Shakespeare's sequence of great comedies continues with *Merchant of Venice*, *Much Ado About Nothing*, *As You Like It*, and *Twelfth Night*. One of his best-loved comedies, *Twelfth Night* is a romantic drama of confusions, comic sequences, and mistaken identities. After a shipwreck, Viola is separated from her twin brother Sebastian—whom she considers to be dead—and is washed ashore on the Illyrian coast. There, she joins the service of Duke Orsino, disguising herself as a young man named Cesario, and falls in love with him. With a perfect combination of romance and reality and excellently crafted characters, *Twelfth Night* has been amusing its audiences for more than four centuries now.

Shakespeare introduced prose comedy in the histories of the late 1590s—*Henry IV, part one* and *part two, and Henry V*—after the lyrical *Richard II*. *Julius Caesar* introduced a new kind of drama. Shakespeare wrote the so-called 'problem plays' in the early 17th century. *Measure for Measure*, *Troilus and Cressida*, and *All's Well that Ends Well* being a few of them. Until about 1608, he mainly wrote tragedies including *Hamlet*, *Othello*, *King Lear*, and *Macbeth*.

Antony and Cleopatra and *Coriolanus*—his last major tragedies, contain some of his finest poetry. Shakespeare wrote tragicomedies, also known as romances, in his last phase. These include *Cymbeline*, *The Winter's Tale*, and *The Tempest*, as well as the collaboration *Pericles, Prince of Tyre*.

A true genius, Shakespeare's popular characters and plots are studied, performed, reinterpreted, and discussed till today. William Shakespeare, known as the English national poet, is considered the greatest dramatist of all time.

Contents

Characters of the Play

ORSINO, Duke of Illyria.

SEBASTIAN, brother to Viola.

ANTONIO, a sea captain, friend to Sebastian.

A Sea Captain, friend to Viola.

VALENTINE and CURIO, gentlemen attending on the Duke.

SIR TOBY BELCH, uncle to Olivia.

SIR ANDREW AGUECHEEK.

MALVOLIO, steward to Olivia.

FABIAN and FESTE, a Clown, servants to Olivia.

OLIVIA.

VIOLA.

MARIA, Olivia's woman.

Lords, Priests, Sailors, Officers, Musicians, and other Attendants.

Scene: A city in Illyria, and the sea-coast near it.

ACT I

Scene I. Duke Orsino's Palace.

Enter Duke Orsino, Curio, and other Lords; Musicians attending

DUKE ORSINO

If music be the food of love, play on;
Give me excess of it, that, surfeiting,
The appetite may sicken, and so die.
That strain again! It had a dying fall:
O, it came o'er my ear like the sweet sound,
That breathes upon a bank of violets,
Stealing and giving odour! Enough; no more:
'Tis not so sweet now as it was before.
O spirit of love! How quick and fresh art thou,
That, notwithstanding thy capacity

Receiveth as the sea, nought enters there,
Of what validity and pitch soe'er,
But falls into abatement and low price,
Even in a minute: so full of shapes is fancy
That it alone is high fantastical.

CURIO

Will you go hunt, my lord?

DUKE ORSINO

What, Curio?

CURIO

The hart.

DUKE ORSINO

Why, so I do, the noblest that I have:
O, when mine eyes did see Olivia first,
Methought she purged the air of pestilence!
That instant was I turn'd into a hart;
And my desires, like fell and cruel hounds,
E'er since pursue me.

Enter Valentine

How now! What news from her?

VALENTINE

So please my lord, I might not be admitted;
But from her handmaid do return this answer:
The element itself, till seven years' heat,

Shall not behold her face at ample view;
But, like a cloistress, she will veiled walk
And water once a day her chamber round
With eye-offending brine: all this to season
A brother's dead love, which she would keep fresh
And lasting in her sad remembrance.

DUKE ORSINO

O, she that hath a heart of that fine frame
To pay this debt of love but to a brother,
How will she love, when the rich golden shaft
Hath kill'd the flock of all affections else
That live in her; when liver, brain and heart,
These sovereign thrones, are all supplied, and fill'd
Her sweet perfections with one self king!
Away before me to sweet beds of flowers:
Love-thoughts lie rich when canopied with bowers.

Exeunt

Scene II. The Sea-Coast.

Enter Viola, a Captain, and Sailors

VIOLA

What country, friends, is this?

CAPTAIN

This is Illyria, lady.

VIOLA

And what should I do in Illyria?
My brother he is in Elysium.
Perchance he is not drown'd: what think you, sailors?

CAPTAIN

It is perchance that you yourself were saved.

VIOLA

O my poor brother! And so perchance may he be.

CAPTAIN

True, madam: and, to comfort you with chance,
Assure yourself, after our ship did split,
When you and those poor number saved with you
Hung on our driving boat, I saw your brother,
Most provident in peril, bind himself,
Courage and hope both teaching him the practice,
To a strong mast that lived upon the sea;
Where, like Arion on the dolphin's back,
I saw him hold acquaintance with the waves
So long as I could see.

VIOLA

For saying so, there's gold:
Mine own escape unfoldeth to my hope,
Whereto thy speech serves for authority,
The like of him. Know'st thou this country?

CAPTAIN

Ay, madam, well; for I was bred and born
Not three hours' travel from this very place.

VIOLA

Who governs here?

CAPTAIN

A noble duke, in nature as in name.

VIOLA

What is the name?

CAPTAIN

Orsino.

VIOLA

Orsino! I have heard my father name him:
He was a bachelor then.

CAPTAIN

And so is now, or was so very late;
For but a month ago I went from hence,
And then 'twas fresh in murmur—as, you know,
What great ones do the less will prattle of—
That he did seek the love of fair Olivia.

VIOLA

What's she?

CAPTAIN

A virtuous maid, the daughter of a count

That died some twelvemonth since, then leaving her
In the protection of his son, her brother,
Who shortly also died: for whose dear love,
They say, she hath abjured the company
And sight of men.

VIOLA

O that I served that lady
And might not be delivered to the world,
Till I had made mine own occasion mellow,
What my estate is!

CAPTAIN

That were hard to compass;
Because she will admit no kind of suit,
No, not the duke's.

VIOLA

There is a fair behavior in thee, captain;
And though that nature with a beauteous wall
Doth oft close in pollution, yet of thee
I will believe thou hast a mind that suits
With this thy fair and outward character.
I prithee, and I'll pay thee bounteously,
Conceal me what I am, and be my aid
For such disguise as haply shall become

The form of my intent. I'll serve this duke:
Thou shall present me as an eunuch to him:
It may be worth thy pains; for I can sing
And speak to him in many sorts of music
That will allow me very worth his service.
What else may hap to time I will commit;
Only shape thou thy silence to my wit.

CAPTAIN

Be you his eunuch, and your mute I'll be:
When my tongue blabs, then let mine eyes not see.

VIOLA

I thank thee: lead me on.

Exeunt

Scene III. Olivia's House.

Enter Sir Toby Belch and Maria

SIR TOBY BELCH

What a plague means my niece, to take the death of her brother thus? I am sure care's an enemy to life.

MARIA

By my troth, Sir Toby, you must come in earlier o' nights: your cousin, my lady, takes great exceptions to your ill hours.

SIR TOBY BELCH

Why, let her except, before excepted.

MARIA

Ay, but you must confine yourself within the modest limits of order.

SIR TOBY BELCH

Confine! I'll confine myself no finer than I am: these clothes are good enough to drink in; and so be these boots too: an they be not, let them hang themselves in their own straps.

MARIA

That quaffing and drinking will undo you: I heard my lady talk of it yesterday; and of a foolish knight that you brought in one night here to be her wooer.

SIR TOBY BELCH

Who, Sir Andrew Aguecheek?

MARIA

Ay, he.

SIR TOBY BELCH

He's as tall a man as any's in Illyria.

MARIA

What's that to the purpose?

SIR TOBY BELCH

Why, he has three thousand ducats a year.

MARIA

Ay, but he'll have but a year in all these ducats: he's a very fool and a prodigal.

SIR TOBY BELCH

Fie, that you'll say so! He plays o' the viol-de-gamboys, and speaks three or four languages word for word without book, and hath all the good gifts of nature.

MARIA

He hath indeed, almost natural: for besides that he's a fool, he's a great quarreller: and but that he hath the gift of a coward, to allay the gust he hath in quarrelling, 'tis thought among the prudent, he would quickly have the gift of a grave.

SIR TOBY BELCH

By this hand, they are scoundrels and subtractors that say so of him. Who are they?

MARIA

They that add, moreover, he's drunk nightly in your company.

SIR TOBY BELCH

With drinking healths to my niece: I'll drink to her as long as there is a passage in my throat and drink in Illyria: he's a coward and a coystrill that will not drink to my niece till his brains turn o' the toe like a parish-top. What, wench! *Castiliano vulgo*! For here comes Sir Andrew Agueface.

Enter Sir Andrew

SIR ANDREW

Sir Toby Belch! How now, Sir Toby Belch!

SIR TOBY BELCH

Sweet Sir Andrew!

SIR ANDREW

Bless you, fair shrew.

MARIA

And you too, sir.

SIR TOBY BELCH

Accost, Sir Andrew, accost.

SIR ANDREW

What's that?

SIR TOBY BELCH

My niece's chambermaid.

SIR ANDREW

Good Mistress Accost, I desire better acquaintance.

MARIA

My name is Mary, sir.

SIR ANDREW

Good Mistress Mary Accost—

SIR TOBY BELCH

You mistake, knight; 'accost' is front her, board her, woo her, assail her.

SIR ANDREW

By my troth, I would not undertake her in this company. Is that the meaning of 'accost'?

MARIA

Fare you well, gentlemen.

SIR TOBY BELCH

An thou let part so, Sir Andrew, would thou mightst never draw sword again.

SIR ANDREW

An you part so, mistress, I would I might never draw sword again. Fair lady, do you think you have fools in hand?

MARIA

Sir, I have not you by the hand.

SIR ANDREW

Marry, but you shall have; and here's my hand.

MARIA

Now, sir, 'thought is free:' I pray you, bring your hand to the buttery-bar and let it drink.

SIR ANDREW

Wherefore, sweet-heart? What's your metaphor?

MARIA

It's dry, sir.

SIR ANDREW

Why, I think so: I am not such an ass but I can keep my hand dry. But what's your jest?

MARIA

A dry jest, sir.

SIR ANDREW

Are you full of them?

MARIA

Ay, sir, I have them at my fingers' ends: marry, now I let go your hand, I am barren.

Exit Maria.

SIR TOBY BELCH

O knight thou lackest a cup of canary: when did I see thee so put down?

SIR ANDREW

Never in your life, I think; unless you see canary put me down. Methinks sometimes I have no more wit than a Christian or an ordinary man has: but I am a great eater of beef and I believe that does harm to my wit.

SIR TOBY BELCH

No question.

SIR ANDREW

An I thought that, I'ld forswear it. I'll ride home to-morrow, Sir Toby.

SIR TOBY BELCH

Pourquoi, my dear knight?

SIR ANDREW

What is '*Pourquoi*'? Do or not do? I would I had bestowed that time in the tongues that I have in fencing, dancing and bear-baiting: O, had I but followed the arts!

SIR TOBY BELCH

Then hadst thou had an excellent head of hair.

SIR ANDREW

Why, would that have mended my hair?

SIR TOBY BELCH

Past question; for thou seest it will not curl by nature.

SIR ANDREW

But it becomes me well enough, does't not?

SIR TOBY BELCH

Excellent; it hangs like flax on a distaff; and I hope to see a housewife take thee between her legs and spin it off.

SIR ANDREW

Faith, I'll home to-morrow, Sir Toby: your niece will

not be seen; or if she be, it's four to one she'll none of me: the count himself here hard by woos her.

SIR TOBY BELCH

She'll none o' the count: she'll not match above her degree, neither in estate, years, nor wit; I have heard her swear't. Tut, there's life in't, man.

SIR ANDREW

I'll stay a month longer. I am a fellow o' the strangest mind i' the world; I delight in masques and revels sometimes altogether.

SIR TOBY BELCH

Art thou good at these kickshawses, knight?

SIR ANDREW

As any man in Illyria, whatsoever he be, under the degree of my betters; and yet I will not compare with an old man.

SIR TOBY BELCH

What is thy excellence in a galliard, knight?

SIR ANDREW

Faith, I can cut a caper.

SIR TOBY BELCH

And I can cut the mutton to't.

SIR ANDREW

And I think I have the back-trick simply as strong as any man in Illyria.

SIR TOBY BELCH

Wherefore are these things hid? Wherefore have these gifts a curtain before 'em? Are they like to take dust, like Mistress Mall's picture? Why dost thou not go to church in a galliard and come home in a coranto? My very walk should be a jig; I would not so much as make water but in a sink-a-pace. What dost thou mean? Is it a world to hide virtues in? I did think, by the excellent constitution of thy leg, it was formed under the star of a galliard.

SIR ANDREW

Ay, 'tis strong, and it does indifferent well in a flame-coloured stock. Shall we set about some revels?

SIR TOBY BELCH

What shall we do else? Were we not born under Taurus?

SIR ANDREW

Taurus! That's sides and heart.

SIR TOBY BELCH

No, sir; it is legs and thighs. Let me see the caper; ha, higher: ha, ha, excellent!

Exeunt

Scene IV. Duke Orsino's Palace.

Enter Valentine and Viola in Man's Attire

VALENTINE

If the duke continue these favours towards you, Cesario, you are like to be much advanced: he hath known you but three days, and already you are no stranger.

VIOLA

You either fear his humour or my negligence, that you call in question the continuance of his love: is he inconstant, sir, in his favours?

VALENTINE

No, believe me.

VIOLA

I thank you. Here comes the count.

Enter Duke Orsino, Curio, and Attendants

DUKE ORSINO

Who saw Cesario, ho?

VIOLA

On your attendance, my lord; here.

DUKE ORSINO

Stand you a while aloof, Cesario,

Thou know'st no less but all; I have unclasp'd

To thee the book even of my secret soul:

Therefore, good youth, address thy gait unto her;
Be not denied access, stand at her doors,
And tell them, there thy fixed foot shall grow
Till thou have audience.

VIOLA

Sure, my noble lord,
If she be so abandon'd to her sorrow
As it is spoke, she never will admit me.

DUKE ORSINO

Be clamorous and leap all civil bounds
Rather than make unprofited return.

VIOLA

Say I do speak with her, my lord, what then?

DUKE ORSINO

O, then unfold the passion of my love,
Surprise her with discourse of my dear faith:
It shall become thee well to act my woes;
She will attend it better in thy youth
Than in a nuncio's of more grave aspect.

VIOLA

I think not so, my lord.

DUKE ORSINO

Dear lad, believe it;
For they shall yet belie thy happy years,

That say thou art a man: Diana's lip
Is not more smooth and rubious; thy small pipe
Is as the maiden's organ, shrill and sound,
And all is semblative a woman's part.
I know thy constellation is right apt
For this affair. Some four or five attend him;
All, if you will; for I myself am best
When least in company. Prosper well in this,
And thou shalt live as freely as thy lord,
To call his fortunes thine.

VIOLA

I'll do my best
To woo your lady: [*Aside*] yet, a barful strife!
Whoe'er I woo, myself would be his wife.

Exeunt

Scene V. Olivia's House.

Enter Maria and Clown

MARIA

Nay, either tell me where thou hast been, or I will not open my lips so wide as a bristle may enter in way of thy excuse: my lady will hang thee for thy absence.

CLOWN

Let her hang me: he that is well hanged in this world needs to fear no colours.

MARIA

Make that good.

CLOWN

He shall see none to fear.

MARIA

A good lenten answer: I can tell thee where that saying was born, of 'I fear no colours.'

CLOWN

Where, good Mistress Mary?

MARIA

In the wars; and that may you be bold to say in your foolery.

CLOWN

Well, God give them wisdom that have it; and those that are fools, let them use their talents.

MARIA

Yet you will be hanged for being so long absent; or, to be turned away, is not that as good as a hanging to you?

CLOWN

Many a good hanging prevents a bad marriage; and, for turning away, let summer bear it out.

MARIA

You are resolute, then?

CLOWN

Not so, neither; but I am resolved on two points.

MARIA

That if one break, the other will hold; or, if both break, your gaskins fall.

CLOWN

Apt, in good faith; very apt. Well, go thy way; if Sir Toby would leave drinking, thou wert as witty a piece of Eve's flesh as any in Illyria.

MARIA

Peace, you rogue, no more o' that. Here comes my lady: make your excuse wisely, you were best.

Exit

CLOWN

Wit, an't be thy will, put me into good fooling! Those wits, that think they have thee, do very oft prove fools; and I, that am sure I lack thee, may pass for a wise man. For what says Quinapalus? 'Better a witty fool, than a foolish wit.'

Enter Olivia with Malvolio

God bless thee, lady!

OLIVIA

Take the fool away.

CLOWN

Do you not hear, fellows? Take away the lady.

OLIVIA

Go to, you're a dry fool; I'll no more of you: besides, you grow dishonest.

CLOWN

Two faults, madonna, that drink and good counsel will amend: for give the dry fool drink, then is the fool not dry: bid the dishonest man mend himself; if he mend, he is no longer dishonest; if he cannot, let the botcher mend him. Any thing that's mended is but patched: virtue that transgresses is but patched with sin; and sin that amends is but patched with virtue. If that this simple syllogism will serve, so; if it will not, what remedy? As there is no true cuckold but calamity, so beauty's a flower. The lady bade take away the fool; therefore, I say again, take her away.

OLIVIA

Sir, I bade them take away you.

CLOWN

Misprision in the highest degree! Lady, *cucullus non facit monachum*; that's as much to say as I wear not motley in my brain. Good madonna, give me leave to prove you a fool.

OLIVIA

Can you do it?

CLOWN

Dexterously, good madonna.

OLIVIA

Make your proof.

CLOWN

I must catechise you for it, madonna: good my mouse of virtue, answer me.

OLIVIA

Well, sir, for want of other idleness, I'll bide your proof.

CLOWN

Good madonna, why mournest thou?

OLIVIA

Good fool, for my brother's death.

CLOWN

I think his soul is in hell, madonna.

OLIVIA

I know his soul is in heaven, fool.

CLOWN

The more fool, madonna, to mourn for your brother's soul being in heaven. Take away the fool, gentlemen.

OLIVIA

What think you of this fool, Malvolio? Doth he not mend?

MALVOLIO

Yes, and shall do till the pangs of death shake him: infirmity, that decays the wise, doth ever make the better fool.

CLOWN

God send you, sir, a speedy infirmity, for the better increasing your folly! Sir Toby will be sworn that I am no fox; but he will not pass his word for two pence that you are no fool.

OLIVIA

How say you to that, Malvolio?

MALVOLIO

I marvel your ladyship takes delight in such a barren rascal: I saw him put down the other day with an ordinary fool that has no more brain than a stone. Look you now, he's out of his guard already; unless you laugh and minister occasion to him, he is gagged.

I protest, I take these wise men, that crow so at these set kind of fools, no better than the fools' zanies.

OLIVIA

Oh, you are sick of self-love, Malvolio, and taste with a distempered appetite. To be generous, guiltless and of free disposition, is to take those things for bird-bolts that you deem cannon-bullets: there is no slander in an allowed fool, though he do nothing but rail; nor no railing in a known discreet man, though he do nothing but reprove.

CLOWN

Now Mercury indue thee with leasing, for thou speakest well of fools!

Re-enter Maria

MARIA

Madam, there is at the gate a young gentleman much desires to speak with you.

OLIVIA

From the Count Orsino, is it?

MARIA

I know not, madam: 'tis a fair young man, and well attended.

OLIVIA

Who of my people hold him in delay?

MARIA

Sir Toby, madam, your kinsman.

OLIVIA

Fetch him off, I pray you; he speaks nothing but madman: fie on him!

Exit Maria

Go you, Malvolio: if it be a suit from the count, I am sick, or not at home; what you will, to dismiss it.

Exit Malvolio

Now you see, sir, how your fooling grows old, and people dislike it.

CLOWN

Thou hast spoke for us, madonna, as if thy eldest son should be a fool; whose skull Jove cram with brains! For—here he comes—one of thy kin has a most weak *pia mater*.

Enter Sir Toby Belch

OLIVIA

By mine honour, half drunk. What is he at the gate, cousin?

SIR TOBY BELCH

A gentleman.

OLIVIA

A gentleman! What gentleman?

SIR TOBY BELCH

'Tis a gentle man here—a plague o' these pickle-herring! How now, sot!

CLOWN

Good Sir Toby!

OLIVIA

Cousin, cousin, how have you come so early by this lethargy?

SIR TOBY BELCH

Lechery! I defy lechery. There's one at the gate.

OLIVIA

Ay, marry, what is he?

SIR TOBY BELCH

Let him be the devil, an he will, I care not: give me faith, say I. Well, it's all one.

Exit

OLIVIA

What's a drunken man like, fool?

CLOWN

Like a drowned man, a fool and a mad man: one draught above heat makes him a fool; the second mads him; and a third drowns him.

OLIVIA

Go thou and seek the crowner, and let him sit o'

my coz; for he's in the third degree of drink, he's drowned: go, look after him.

CLOWN

He is but mad yet, madonna; and the fool shall look to the madman.

Exit

Re-enter Malvolio

MALVOLIO

Madam, yond young fellow swears he will speak with you. I told him you were sick; he takes on him to understand so much, and therefore comes to speak with you. I told him you were asleep; he seems to have a foreknowledge of that too, and therefore comes to speak with you. What is to be said to him, lady? He's fortified against any denial.

OLIVIA

Tell him he shall not speak with me.

MALVOLIO

Has been told so; and he says, he'll stand at your door like a sheriff's post, and be the supporter to a bench, but he'll speak with you.

OLIVIA

What kind o' man is he?

MALVOLIO

Why, of mankind.

OLIVIA

What manner of man?

MALVOLIO

Of very ill manner; he'll speak with you, will you or no.

OLIVIA

Of what personage and years is he?

MALVOLIO

Not yet old enough for a man, nor young enough for a boy; as a squash is before 'tis a peascod, or a cooling when 'tis almost an apple: 'tis with him in standing water, between boy and man. He is very well-favoured and he speaks very shrewishly; one would think his mother's milk were scarce out of him.

OLIVIA

Let him approach: call in my gentlewoman.

MALVOLIO

Gentlewoman, my lady calls.

Exit

Re-enter Maria

OLIVIA

Give me my veil: come, throw it o'er my face. We'll once more hear Orsino's embassy.

Enter Viola, and Attendants

VIOLA

The honourable lady of the house, which is she?

OLIVIA

Speak to me; I shall answer for her. Your will?

VIOLA

Most radiant, exquisite and unmatchable beauty—I pray you, tell me if this be the lady of the house, for I never saw her: I would be loath to cast away my speech, for besides that it is excellently well penned, I have taken great pains to con it. Good beauties, let me sustain no scorn; I am very comptible, even to the least sinister usage.

OLIVIA

Whence came you, sir?

VIOLA

I can say little more than I have studied, and that question's out of my part. Good gentle one, give me modest assurance if you be the lady of the house, that I may proceed in my speech.

OLIVIA

Are you a comedian?

VIOLA

No, my profound heart: and yet, by the very fangs of malice I swear, I am not that I play. Are you the lady of the house?

OLIVIA

If I do not usurp myself, I am.

VIOLA

Most certain, if you are she, you do usurp yourself; for what is yours to bestow is not yours to reserve. But this is from my commission: I will on with my speech in your praise, and then show you the heart of my message.

OLIVIA

Come to what is important in't: I forgive you the praise.

VIOLA

Alas, I took great pains to study it, and 'tis poetical.

OLIVIA

It is the more like to be feigned: I pray you, keep it in. I heard you were saucy at my gates, and allowed your approach rather to wonder at you than to hear you. If you be not mad, be gone; if you have reason, be brief: 'tis not that time of moon with me to make one in so skipping a dialogue.

MARIA

Will you hoist sail, sir? Here lies your way.

VIOLA

No, good swabber; I am to hull here a little longer. Some mollification for your giant, sweet lady. Tell me your mind: I am a messenger.

OLIVIA

Sure, you have some hideous matter to deliver, when the courtesy of it is so fearful. Speak your office.

VIOLA

It alone concerns your ear. I bring no overture of war, no taxation of homage: I hold the olive in my hand; my words are as fun of peace as matter.

OLIVIA

Yet you began rudely. What are you? What would you?

VIOLA

The rudeness that hath appeared in me have I learned from my entertainment. What I am, and what I would, are as secret as maidenhead; to your ears, divinity, to any other's, profanation.

OLIVIA

Give us the place alone: we will hear this divinity.

Exeunt Maria and Attendants

Now, sir, what is your text?

VIOLA

Most sweet lady—

OLIVIA

A comfortable doctrine, and much may be said of it. Where lies your text?

VIOLA

In Orsino's bosom.

OLIVIA

In his bosom! In what chapter of his bosom?

VIOLA

To answer by the method, in the first of his heart.

OLIVIA

O, I have read it: it is heresy. Have you no more to say?

VIOLA

Good madam, let me see your face.

OLIVIA

Have you any commission from your lord to negotiate with my face? You are now out of your text: but we will draw the curtain and show you the picture. Look you, sir, such a one I was this present: is't not well done?

Unveiling

VIOLA

Excellently done, if God did all.

OLIVIA

'Tis in grain, sir; 'twill endure wind and weather.

VIOLA

'Tis beauty truly blent, whose red and white
Nature's own sweet and cunning hand laid on:
Lady, you are the cruell'st she alive,
If you will lead these graces to the grave
And leave the world no copy.

OLIVIA

O, sir, I will not be so hard-hearted; I will give out divers schedules of my beauty: it shall be inventoried, and every particle and utensil labelled to my will: as, item, two lips, indifferent red; item, two grey eyes, with lids to them; item, one neck, one chin, and so forth. Were you sent hither to praise me?

VIOLA

I see you what you are, you are too proud;
But, if you were the devil, you are fair.
My lord and master loves you: O, such love

Could be but recompensed, though you were crown'd
The nonpareil of beauty!

OLIVIA

How does he love me?

VIOLA

With adorations, fertile tears,
With groans that thunder love, with sighs of fire.

OLIVIA

Your lord does know my mind; I cannot love him:
Yet I suppose him virtuous, know him noble,
Of great estate, of fresh and stainless youth;
In voices well divulged, free, learn'd and valiant;
And in dimension and the shape of nature
A gracious person: but yet I cannot love him;
He might have took his answer long ago.

VIOLA

If I did love you in my master's flame,
With such a suffering, such a deadly life,
In your denial I would find no sense;
I would not understand it.

OLIVIA

Why, what would you?

VIOLA

Make me a willow cabin at your gate,
And call upon my soul within the house;
Write loyal cantons of contemned love
And sing them loud even in the dead of night;
Halloo your name to the reverberate hills
And make the babbling gossip of the air
Cry out 'Olivia!' O, You should not rest
Between the elements of air and earth,
But you should pity me!

OLIVIA

You might do much. What is your parentage?

VIOLA

Above my fortunes, yet my state is well:
I am a gentleman.

OLIVIA

Get you to your lord;
I cannot love him: let him send no more;
Unless, perchance, you come to me again,
To tell me how he takes it. Fare you well:
I thank you for your pains: spend this for me.

VIOLA

I am no fee'd post, lady; keep your purse:
My master, not myself, lacks recompense.

Love make his heart of flint that you shall love;
And let your fervor, like my master's, be
Placed in contempt! Farewell, fair cruelty.

Exit

OLIVIA

'What is your parentage?'
'Above my fortunes, yet my state is well:
I am a gentleman.' I'll be sworn thou art;
Thy tongue, thy face, thy limbs, actions and spirit,
Do give thee five-fold blazon: not too fast: soft, soft!
Unless the master were the man. How now!
Even so quickly may one catch the plague?
Methinks I feel this youth's perfections
With an invisible and subtle stealth
To creep in at mine eyes. Well, let it be.
What ho, Malvolio!

Re-enter Malvolio

MALVOLIO

Here, madam, at your service.

OLIVIA

Run after that same peevish messenger,
The county's man: he left this ring behind him,
Would I or not: tell him I'll none of it.

Desire him not to flatter with his lord,
Nor hold him up with hopes; I am not for him:
If that the youth will come this way to-morrow,
I'll give him reasons for't: hie thee, Malvolio.

MALVOLIO

Madam, I will.

Exit

OLIVIA

I do I know not what, and fear to find
Mine eye too great a flatterer for my mind.
Fate, show thy force: ourselves we do not owe;
What is decreed must be, and be this so.

Exit

***

ACT II

Scene I. The sea-coast.

Enter Antonio and Sebastian

ANTONIO

Will you stay no longer? Nor will you not that I go with you?

SEBASTIAN

By your patience, no. My stars shine darkly over me: the malignancy of my fate might perhaps distemper yours; therefore I shall crave of you your leave that I may bear my evils alone: it were a bad recompense for your love, to lay any of them on you.

ANTONIO

Let me yet know of you whither you are bound.

SEBASTIAN

No, sooth, sir: my determinate voyage is mere extravagancy. But I perceive in you so excellent a touch of modesty, that you will not extort from me what I am willing to keep in; therefore it charges me in manners the rather to express myself. You must know of me then, Antonio, my name is Sebastian, which I called Roderigo. My father was that Sebastian of Messaline, whom I know you have heard of. He left behind him myself and a sister, both born in an hour: if the heavens had been pleased, would we had so ended! But you, sir, altered that; for some hour before you took me from the breach of the sea was my sister drowned.

ANTONIO

Alas the day!

SEBASTIAN

A lady, sir, though it was said she much resembled me, was yet of many accounted beautiful: but, though I could not with such estimable wonder overfar believe that, yet thus far I will boldly publish her; she bore a mind that envy could not but call fair. She is drowned already, sir, with salt water, though I seem to drown her remembrance again with more.

ANTONIO

Pardon me, sir, your bad entertainment.

SEBASTIAN

O good Antonio, forgive me your trouble.

ANTONIO

If you will not murder me for my love, let me be your servant.

SEBASTIAN

If you will not undo what you have done, that is, kill

him whom you have recovered, desire it not. Fare ye well at once: my bosom is full of kindness, and I am yet so near the manners of my mother, that upon the least occasion more mine eyes will tell tales of me. I am bound to the Count Orsino's court: farewell.

Exit

ANTONIO

The gentleness of all the gods go with thee!
I have many enemies in Orsino's court,
Else would I very shortly see thee there.
But, come what may, I do adore thee so,
That danger shall seem sport, and I will go.

Exit

Scene II. A street.

Enter Viola, Malvolio following

MALVOLIO

Were not you even now with the Countess Olivia?

VIOLA

Even now, sir; on a moderate pace I have since arrived but hither.

MALVOLIO

She returns this ring to you, sir: you might have saved me my pains, to have taken it away yourself.

She adds, moreover, that you should put your lord into a desperate assurance she will none of him: and one thing more, that you be never so hardy to come again in his affairs, unless it be to report your lord's taking of this. Receive it so.

VIOLA

She took the ring of me: I'll none of it.

MALVOLIO

Come, sir, you peevishly threw it to her; and her will is, it should be so returned: if it be worth stooping for, there it lies in your eye; if not, be it his that finds it.

Exit

VIOLA

I left no ring with her: what means this lady?
Fortune forbid my outside have not charm'd her!
She made good view of me; indeed, so much,
That sure methought her eyes had lost her tongue,
For she did speak in starts distractedly.
She loves me, sure; the cunning of her passion
Invites me in this churlish messenger.
None of my lord's ring! Why, he sent her none.
I am the man: if it be so, as 'tis,
Poor lady, she were better love a dream.

Disguise, I see, thou art a wickedness,
Wherein the pregnant enemy does much.
How easy is it for the proper-false
In women's waxen hearts to set their forms!
Alas, our frailty is the cause, not we!
For such as we are made of, such we be.
How will this fadge? My master loves her dearly;
And I, poor monster, fond as much on him;
And she, mistaken, seems to dote on me.
What will become of this? As I am man,
My state is desperate for my master's love;
As I am woman—now alas the day!—
What thriftless sighs shall poor Olivia breathe!
O time! Thou must untangle this, not I;
It is too hard a knot for me to untie!

Exit

Scene III. Olivia's house.

Enter Sir Toby Belch and Sir Andrew

SIR TOBY BELCH

Approach, Sir Andrew: not to be abed after midnight is to be up betimes; and '*diluculo surgere*,' thou know'st—

SIR ANDREW

Nay, my troth, I know not: but I know, to be up late is to be up late.

SIR TOBY BELCH

A false conclusion: I hate it as an unfilled can. To be up after midnight and to go to bed then, is early: so that to go to bed after midnight is to go to bed betimes. Does not our life consist of the four elements?

SIR ANDREW

Faith, so they say; but I think it rather consists of eating and drinking.

SIR TOBY BELCH

Thou'rt a scholar; let us therefore eat and drink. Marian, I say! A stoup of wine!

Enter Clown

SIR ANDREW

Here comes the fool, i' faith.

CLOWN

How now, my hearts! Did you never see the picture of 'we three'?

SIR TOBY BELCH

Welcome, ass. Now let's have a catch.

SIR ANDREW

By my troth, the fool has an excellent breast. I had rather than forty shillings I had such a leg, and so sweet a breath to sing, as the fool has. In sooth, thou wast in very gracious fooling last night, when thou spokest of Pigrogromitus, of the Vapians passing the equinoctial of Queubus: 'twas very good, i' faith. I sent thee sixpence for thy leman: hadst it?

CLOWN

I did impeticos thy gratillity; for Malvolio's nose is no whipstock: my lady has a white hand, and the Myrmidons are no bottle-ale houses.

SIR ANDREW

Excellent! Why, this is the best fooling, when all is done. Now, a song.

SIR TOBY BELCH

Come on; there is sixpence for you: let's have a song.

SIR ANDREW

There's a testril of me too: if one knight give a—

CLOWN

Would you have a love-song, or a song of good life?

SIR TOBY BELCH

A love-song, a love-song.

SIR ANDREW

Ay, ay: I care not for good life.

CLOWN

[*Sings*] *O mistress mine, where are you roaming?*

O, stay and hear; your true love's coming,

That can sing both high and low:

Trip no further, pretty sweeting;

Journeys end in lovers meeting,

Every wise man's son doth know.

SIR ANDREW

Excellent good, i' faith.

SIR TOBY BELCH

Good, good.

CLOWN

[*Sings*] *What is love? 'Tis not hereafter;*

Present mirth hath present laughter;

What's to come is still unsure:

In delay there lies no plenty;

Then come kiss me, sweet and twenty,

Youth's a stuff will not endure.

SIR ANDREW

A mellifluous voice, as I am true knight.

SIR TOBY BELCH

A contagious breath.

SIR ANDREW

Very sweet and contagious, i' faith.

SIR TOBY BELCH

To hear by the nose, it is dulcet in contagion. But shall we make the welkin dance indeed? Shall we rouse the night-owl in a catch that will draw three souls out of one weaver? Shall we do that?

SIR ANDREW

An you love me, let's do't: I am dog at a catch.

CLOWN

By'r lady, sir, and some dogs will catch well.

SIR ANDREW

Most certain. Let our catch be, '*Thou knave.*'

CLOWN

'*Hold thy peace, thou knave,*' knight? I shall be constrained in't to call thee knave, knight.

SIR ANDREW

'Tis not the first time I have constrained one to call me knave. Begin, fool: it begins '*Hold thy peace.*'

CLOWN

I shall never begin if I hold my peace.

SIR ANDREW

Good, i' faith. Come, begin.

Catch sung

Enter MARIA

MARIA

What a caterwauling do you keep here! If my lady have not called up her steward Malvolio and bid him turn you out of doors, never trust me.

SIR TOBY BELCH

My lady's a Cataian, we are politicians, Malvolio's a Peg-a-Ramsey, and '*Three merry men be we.*' Am not I consanguineous? Am I not of her blood? Tillyvally. Lady!

[*Sings*] '*There dwelt a man in Babylon, lady, lady!*'

CLOWN

Beshrew me, the knight's in admirable fooling.

SIR ANDREW

Ay, he does well enough if he be disposed, and so do I too: he does it with a better grace, but I do it more natural.

SIR TOBY BELCH

[*Sings*] '*O, the twelfth day of December,*'—

MARIA

For the love o' God, peace!

Enter Malvolio

MALVOLIO

My masters, are you mad? Or what are you? Have ye no wit, manners, nor honesty, but to gabble like tinkers at this time of night? Do ye make an alehouse of my lady's house, that ye squeak out your coziers' catches without any mitigation or remorse of voice? Is there no respect of place, persons, nor time in you?

SIR TOBY BELCH

We did keep time, sir, in our catches. Sneck up!

MALVOLIO

Sir Toby, I must be round with you. My lady bade me tell you, that, though she harbours you as her kinsman, she's nothing allied to your disorders. If you can separate yourself and your misdemeanors, you are welcome to the house; if not, an it would please you to take leave of her, she is very willing to bid you farewell.

SIR TOBY BELCH

'Farewell, dear heart, since I must needs be gone.'

MARIA

Nay, good Sir Toby.

CLOWN

'His eyes do show his days are almost done.'

MALVOLIO

Is't even so?

SIR TOBY BELCH

'But I will never die.'

CLOWN

Sir Toby, there you lie.

MALVOLIO

This is much credit to you.

SIR TOBY BELCH

'*Shall I bid him go?*'

CLOWN

'*What an if you do?*'

SIR TOBY BELCH

'*Shall I bid him go, and spare not?*'

CLOWN

'*O no, no, no, no, you dare not.*'

SIR TOBY BELCH

Out o' tune, sir: ye lie. Art any more than a steward? Dost thou think, because thou art virtuous, there shall be no more cakes and ale?

CLOWN

Yes, by Saint Anne, and ginger shall be hot i' the mouth too.

SIR TOBY BELCH

Thou'rt i' the right. Go, sir, rub your chain with crumbs. A stoup of wine, Maria!

MALVOLIO

Mistress Mary, if you prized my lady's favour at any thing more than contempt, you would not give means for this uncivil rule: she shall know of it, by this hand.

Exit

MARIA

Go shake your ears.

SIR ANDREW

'Twere as good a deed as to drink when a man's a-hungry, to challenge him the field, and then to break promise with him and make a fool of him.

SIR TOBY BELCH

Do't, knight: I'll write thee a challenge: or I'll deliver thy indignation to him by word of mouth.

MARIA

Sweet Sir Toby, be patient for tonight: since the youth of the count's was today with thy lady, she is much out of quiet. For Monsieur Malvolio, let me alone with him: if I do not gull him into a nayword, and make him a common recreation, do not think I have wit enough to lie straight in my bed: I know I can do it.

SIR TOBY BELCH

Possess us, possess us; tell us something of him.

MARIA

Marry, sir, sometimes he is a kind of puritan.

SIR ANDREW

O, if I thought that I'ld beat him like a dog!

SIR TOBY BELCH

What, for being a puritan? Thy exquisite reason, dear knight?

SIR ANDREW

I have no exquisite reason for't, but I have reason good enough.

MARIA

The devil a puritan that he is, or any thing constantly, but a time-pleaser; an affectioned ass, that cons state without book and utters it by great swarths: the best persuaded of himself, so crammed, as he thinks, with excellencies, that it is his grounds of faith that all that look on him love him; and on that vice in him will my revenge find notable cause to work.

SIR TOBY BELCH

What wilt thou do?

MARIA

I will drop in his way some obscure epistles of love; wherein, by the colour of his beard, the shape of his leg, the manner of his gait, the expressure of his eye, forehead, and complexion, he shall find himself most feelingly personated. I can write very like my lady your niece: on a forgotten matter we can hardly make distinction of our hands.

SIR TOBY BELCH

Excellent! I smell a device.

SIR ANDREW

I have't in my nose too.

SIR TOBY BELCH

He shall think, by the letters that thou wilt drop, that they come from my niece, and that she's in love with him.

MARIA

My purpose is, indeed, a horse of that colour.

SIR ANDREW

And your horse now would make him an ass.

MARIA

Ass, I doubt not.

SIR ANDREW

O, 'twill be admirable!

MARIA

Sport royal, I warrant you: I know my physic will work with him. I will plant you two, and let the fool make a third, where he shall find the letter: observe his construction of it. For this night, to bed, and dream on the event. Farewell.

Exit

SIR TOBY BELCH

Good night, Penthesilea.

SIR ANDREW

Before me, she's a good wench.

SIR TOBY BELCH

She's a beagle, true-bred, and one that adores me: what o' that?

SIR ANDREW

I was adored once too.

SIR TOBY BELCH

Let's to bed, knight. Thou hadst need send for more money.

SIR ANDREW

If I cannot recover your niece, I am a foul way out.

SIR TOBY BELCH

Send for money, knight: if thou hast her not i' the end, call me cut.

SIR ANDREW

If I do not, never trust me, take it how you will.

SIR TOBY BELCH

Come, come, I'll go burn some sack; 'tis too late to go to bed now: come, knight; come, knight.

Exeunt

Scene IV. Duke Orsino's Palace.

Enter Duke Orsino, Viola, Curio, and Others

DUKE ORSINO

Give me some music. Now, good morrow, friends.
Now, good Cesario, but that piece of song,
That old and antique song we heard last night:
Methought it did relieve my passion much,
More than light airs and recollected terms
Of these most brisk and giddy-paced times:
Come, but one verse.

CURIO

He is not here, so please your lordship that should sing it.

DUKE ORSINO

Who was it?

CURIO

Feste, the jester, my lord; a fool that the lady

Olivia's father took much delight in. He is about the house.

DUKE ORSINO

Seek him out, and play the tune the while.

Exit Curio. Music plays

Come hither, boy: if ever thou shalt love,
In the sweet pangs of it remember me;
For such as I am all true lovers are,
Unstaid and skittish in all motions else,
Save in the constant image of the creature
That is beloved. How dost thou like this tune?

VIOLA

It gives a very echo to the seat
Where Love is throned.

DUKE ORSINO

Thou dost speak masterly:
My life upon't, young though thou art, thine eye
Hath stay'd upon some favour that it loves:
Hath it not, boy?

VIOLA

A little, by your favour.

DUKE ORSINO

What kind of woman is't?

VIOLA

Of your complexion.

DUKE ORSINO

She is not worth thee, then. What years, i' faith?

VIOLA

About your years, my lord.

DUKE ORSINO

Too old by heaven: let still the woman take
An elder than herself: so wears she to him,
So sways she level in her husband's heart:
For, boy, however we do praise ourselves,
Our fancies are more giddy and unfirm,
More longing, wavering, sooner lost and worn,
Than women's are.

VIOLA

I think it well, my lord.

DUKE ORSINO

Then let thy love be younger than thyself,
Or thy affection cannot hold the bent;
For women are as roses, whose fair flower
Being once display'd, doth fall that very hour.

VIOLA

And so they are: alas, that they are so;
To die, even when they to perfection grow!

Re-enter Curio and Clown

DUKE ORSINO

O, fellow, come, the song we had last night.
Mark it, Cesario, it is old and plain;
The spinsters and the knitters in the sun
And the free maids that weave their thread with bones
Do use to chant it: it is silly sooth,
And dallies with the innocence of love,
Like the old age.

CLOWN

Are you ready, sir?

DUKE ORSINO

Ay; prithee, sing.

Music

Song

CLOWN

Come away, come away, death,
And in sad cypress let me be laid;
Fly away, fly away breath;
I am slain by a fair cruel maid.
My shroud of white, stuck all with yew,
O, prepare it!
My part of death, no one so true

Did share it.

Not a flower, not a flower sweet
On my black coffin let there be strown;
Not a friend, not a friend greet
My poor corpse, where my bones shall be thrown:
A thousand thousand sighs to save,
Lay me, O, where
Sad true lover never find my grave,
To weep there!

DUKE ORSINO

There's for thy pains.

CLOWN

No pains, sir: I take pleasure in singing, sir.

DUKE ORSINO

I'll pay thy pleasure then.

CLOWN

Truly, sir, and pleasure will be paid, one time or another.

DUKE ORSINO

Give me now leave to leave thee.

CLOWN

Now, the melancholy god protect thee; and the tailor

make thy doublet of changeable taffeta, for thy mind is a very opal. I would have men of such constancy put to sea, that their business might be every thing and their intent every where; for that's it that always makes a good voyage of nothing. Farewell.

Exit

DUKE ORSINO

Let all the rest give place.

Curio and Attendants retire

Once more, Cesario,
Get thee to yond same sovereign cruelty:
Tell her, my love, more noble than the world,
Prizes not quantity of dirty lands;
The parts that fortune hath bestow'd upon her,
Tell her, I hold as giddily as fortune;
But 'tis that miracle and queen of gems
That nature pranks her in attracts my soul.

VIOLA

But if she cannot love you, sir?

DUKE ORSINO

I cannot be so answer'd.

VIOLA

Sooth, but you must.
Say that some lady, as perhaps there is,

Hath for your love a great a pang of heart
As you have for Olivia: you cannot love her;
You tell her so; must she not then be answer'd?

DUKE ORSINO

There is no woman's sides
Can bide the beating of so strong a passion
As love doth give my heart; no woman's heart
So big, to hold so much; they lack retention
Alas, their love may be call'd appetite,
No motion of the liver, but the palate,
That suffer surfeit, cloyment and revolt;
But mine is all as hungry as the sea,
And can digest as much: make no compare
Between that love a woman can bear me
And that I owe Olivia.

VIOLA

Ay, but I know—

DUKE ORSINO

What dost thou know?

VIOLA

Too well what love women to men may owe:
In faith, they are as true of heart as we.
My father had a daughter loved a man,
As it might be, perhaps, were I a woman,

I should your lordship.

DUKE ORSINO

And what's her history?

VIOLA

A blank, my lord. She never told her love,
But let concealment, like a worm i' the bud,
Feed on her damask cheek: she pined in thought,
And with a green and yellow melancholy
She sat like Patience on a monument,
Smiling at grief. Was not this love indeed?
We men may say more, swear more: but indeed
Our shows are more than will; for still we prove
Much in our vows, but little in our love.

DUKE ORSINO

But died thy sister of her love, my boy?

VIOLA

I am all the daughters of my father's house,
And all the brothers too: and yet I know not.
Sir, shall I to this lady?

DUKE ORSINO

Ay, that's the theme.
To her in haste; give her this jewel; say,
My love can give no place, bide no denay.

Exeunt

Scene V. Olivia's Garden.

Enter Sir Toby Belch, Sir Andrew, and Fabian

SIR TOBY BELCH

Come thy ways, Signior Fabian.

FABIAN

Nay, I'll come: if I lose a scruple of this sport, let me be boiled to death with melancholy.

SIR TOBY BELCH

Wouldst thou not be glad to have the niggardly rascally sheep-biter come by some notable shame?

FABIAN

I would exult, man: you know, he brought me out o' favour with my lady about a bear-baiting here.

SIR TOBY BELCH

To anger him we'll have the bear again; and we will fool him black and blue: shall we not, Sir Andrew?

SIR ANDREW

An we do not, it is pity of our lives.

SIR TOBY BELCH

Here comes the little villain.

Enter Maria

How now, my metal of India!

MARIA

Get ye all three into the box-tree: Malvolio's

coming down this walk: he has been yonder i' the sun practising behavior to his own shadow this half hour: observe him, for the love of mockery; for I know this letter will make a contemplative idiot of him. Close, in the name of jesting! Lie thou there, [*Throws down a letter*] for here comes the trout that must be caught with tickling.

Exit

Enter Malvolio

MALVOLIO

'Tis but fortune; all is fortune. Maria once told me she did affect me: and I have heard herself come thus near, that, should she fancy, it should be one of my complexion. Besides, she uses me with a more exalted respect than any one else that follows her. What should I think on't?

SIR TOBY BELCH

Here's an overweening rogue!

FABIAN

O, peace! Contemplation makes a rare turkey-cock of him: how he jets under his advanced plumes!

SIR ANDREW

'Slight, I could so beat the rogue!

SIR TOBY BELCH

Peace, I say.

MALVOLIO

To be Count Malvolio!

SIR TOBY BELCH

Ah, rogue!

SIR ANDREW

Pistol him, pistol him.

SIR TOBY BELCH

Peace, peace!

MALVOLIO

There is example for't; the lady of the Strachy married the yeoman of the wardrobe.

SIR ANDREW

Fie on him, Jezebel!

FABIAN

O, peace! Now he's deeply in: look how imagination blows him.

MALVOLIO

Having been three months married to her, sitting in my state—

SIR TOBY BELCH

O, for a stone-bow, to hit him in the eye!

MALVOLIO

Calling my officers about me, in my branched velvet gown; having come from a day-bed, where I have left Olivia sleeping—

SIR TOBY BELCH

Fire and brimstone!

FABIAN

O, peace, peace!

MALVOLIO

And then to have the humour of state; and after a demure travel of regard, telling them I know my place as I would they should do theirs, to for my kinsman Toby—

SIR TOBY BELCH

Bolts and shackles!

FABIAN

O peace, peace, peace! Now, now.

MALVOLIO

Seven of my people, with an obedient start, make out for him: I frown the while; and perchance wind up watch, or play with my—some rich jewel. Toby approaches; courtesies there to me—

SIR TOBY BELCH

Shall this fellow live?

FABIAN

Though our silence be drawn from us with cars, yet peace.

MALVOLIO

I extend my hand to him thus, quenching my familiar smile with an austere regard of control—

SIR TOBY BELCH

And does not Toby take you a blow o' the lips then?

MALVOLIO

Saying, 'Cousin Toby, my fortunes having cast me on your niece give me this prerogative of speech,'—

SIR TOBY BELCH

What, what?

MALVOLIO

'You must amend your drunkenness.'

SIR TOBY BELCH

Out, scab!

FABIAN

Nay, patience, or we break the sinews of our plot.

MALVOLIO

'Besides, you waste the treasure of your time with a foolish knight,'—

SIR ANDREW

That's me, I warrant you.

MALVOLIO

'One Sir Andrew,'—

SIR ANDREW

I knew 'twas I; for many do call me fool.

MALVOLIO

What employment have we here?

Taking up the letter

FABIAN

Now is the woodcock near the gin.

SIR TOBY BELCH

O, peace! And the spirit of humour intimate reading aloud to him!

MALVOLIO

By my life, this is my lady's hand these be her very *C's*, her *U's* and her *T's* and thus makes she her great *P's*. It is, in contempt of question, her hand.

SIR ANDREW

Her *C's*, her *U's* and her *T's*: why that?

MALVOLIO

[*Reads*] *'To the unknown beloved, this, and my good wishes:'*—her very phrases! By your leave, wax. Soft! And the impressure her Lucrece, with which she uses to seal: 'tis my lady. To whom should this be?

FABIAN

This wins him, liver and all.

MALVOLIO

[*Reads*] *Jove knows I love: But who?*

Lips, do not move;

No man must know.

'No man must know.' What follows? The numbers altered! 'No man must know:' if this should be thee, Malvolio?

SIR TOBY BELCH

Marry, hang thee, brock!

MALVOLIO

[*Reads*] *I may command where I adore;*

But silence, like a Lucrece knife,

With bloodless stroke my heart doth gore:

M, O, A, I, doth sway my life.

FABIAN

A fustian riddle!

SIR TOBY BELCH

Excellent wench, say I.

MALVOLIO

'*M, O, A, I,* doth sway my life.' Nay, but first, let me see, let me see, let me see.

FABIAN

What dish o' poison has she dressed him!

SIR TOBY BELCH

And with what wing the staniel cheques at it!

MALVOLIO

'I *may command where I adore.*' Why, she may command me: I serve her; she is my lady. Why, this is evident to any formal capacity; there is no obstruction in this: and the end—what should that alphabetical position portend? If I could make that resemble something in me—Softly! M, O, A, I—

SIR TOBY BELCH

O, ay, make up that: he is now at a cold scent.

FABIAN

Sowter will cry upon't for all this, though it be as rank as a fox.

MALVOLIO

M—Malvolio; M—why, that begins my name.

FABIAN

Did not I say he would work it out? The cur is excellent at faults.

MALVOLIO

M—but then there is no consonancy in the sequel; that suffers under probation A should follow but O does.

FABIAN

And O shall end, I hope.

SIR TOBY BELCH

Ay, or I'll cudgel him, and make him cry O!

MALVOLIO

And then *I* comes behind.

FABIAN

Ay, an you had any eye behind you, you might see more detraction at your heels than fortunes before you.

MALVOLIO

M, O, A, I; this simulation is not as the former: and yet, to crush this a little, it would bow to me, for every one of these letters are in my name. Soft! Here follows prose.

[*Reads*] *'If this fall into thy hand, revolve. In my stars I am above thee; but be not afraid of greatness: some are born great, some achieve greatness, and some have greatness thrust upon 'em. Thy Fates open their hands; let thy blood and spirit embrace them; and, to inure thyself to what thou art like to be, cast thy humble slough and appear fresh. Be opposite with a kinsman, surly with servants; let thy tongue tang arguments of state; put thyself into the trick of singularity: she thus advises thee that sighs for thee. Remember who commended thy yellow stockings, and wished to see thee ever cross-gartered: I say, remember. Go to, thou art made, if thou desirest to be so; if not, let me see thee a steward still, the fellow of servants, and not worthy to touch Fortune's fingers. Farewell. She that would alter services with thee,*

The Fortunate-Unhappy.'

Daylight and champaign discovers not more: this is open. I will be proud, I will read politic authors, I will baffle Sir Toby, I will wash off gross acquaintance, I will be point-devise the very man. I do not now fool myself, to let imagination jade me; for every reason excites to this, that my lady loves me. She did commend my yellow stockings of late, she did praise my leg being cross-gartered; and in this she manifests herself to my love, and with a kind of injunction drives me to these habits of her liking. I thank my stars I am happy. I will be strange, stout, in yellow stockings, and cross-gartered, even with the swiftness of putting on. Jove and my stars be praised! Here is yet a postscript.

[*Reads*] *'Thou canst not choose but know who I am. If thou entertainest my love, let it appear in thy smiling; thy smiles become thee well; therefore in my presence still smile, dear my sweet, I prithee.'*

Jove, I thank thee: I will smile; I will do everything that thou wilt have me.

Exit

FABIAN

I will not give my part of this sport for a pension of thousands to be paid from the Sophy.

SIR TOBY BELCH

I could marry this wench for this device.

SIR ANDREW

So could I too.

SIR TOBY BELCH

And ask no other dowry with her but such another jest.

SIR ANDREW

Nor I neither.

FABIAN

Here comes my noble gull-catcher.

Re-enter Maria

SIR TOBY BELCH

Wilt thou set thy foot o' my neck?

SIR ANDREW

Or o' mine either?

SIR TOBY BELCH

Shall I play my freedom at tray-trip, and become thy bond-slave?

SIR ANDREW

I' faith, or I either?

SIR TOBY BELCH

Why, thou hast put him in such a dream, that when the image of it leaves him he must run mad.

MARIA

Nay, but say true; does it work upon him?

SIR TOBY BELCH

Like aqua-vitae with a midwife.

MARIA

If you will then see the fruits of the sport, mark his first approach before my lady: he will come to her in yellow stockings, and 'tis a colour she abhors, and cross-gartered, a fashion she detests; and he will smile upon her, which will now be so unsuitable to her disposition, being addicted to a melancholy as she is, that it cannot but turn him into a notable contempt. If you will see it, follow me.

SIR TOBY BELCH

To the gates of Tartar, thou most excellent devil of wit!

SIR ANDREW

I'll make one too.

Exeunt

***

ACT III

Scene I. Olivia's Garden.

Enter Viola, and Clown with a tabour

VIOLA

Save thee, friend, and thy music: dost thou live by thy tabour?

CLOWN

No, sir, I live by the church.

VIOLA

Art thou a churchman?

CLOWN

No such matter, sir: I do live by the church; for I do live at my house, and my house doth stand by the church.

VIOLA

So thou mayst say, the king lies by a beggar, if a beggar dwell near him; or, the church stands by thy tabour, if thy tabour stand by the church.

CLOWN

You have said, sir. To see this age! A sentence is but a cheveril glove to a good wit: how quickly the wrong side may be turned outward!

VIOLA

Nay, that's certain; they that dally nicely with words may quickly make them wanton.

CLOWN

I would, therefore, my sister had had no name, sir.

VIOLA

Why, man?

CLOWN

Why, sir, her name's a word; and to dally with that word might make my sister wanton. But indeed words are very rascals since bonds disgraced them.

VIOLA

Thy reason, man?

CLOWN

Troth, sir, I can yield you none without words; and words are grown so false, I am loath to prove reason with them.

VIOLA

I warrant thou art a merry fellow and carest for nothing.

CLOWN

Not so, sir, I do care for something; but in my conscience, sir, I do not care for you: if that be to care for nothing, sir, I would it would make you invisible.

VIOLA

Art not thou the Lady Olivia's fool?

CLOWN

No, indeed, sir; the Lady Olivia has no folly: she will keep no fool, sir, till she be married; and fools are as like husbands as pilchards are to herrings; the husband's the bigger: I am indeed not her fool, but her corrupter of words.

VIOLA

I saw thee late at the Count Orsino's.

CLOWN

Foolery, sir, does walk about the orb like the sun, it shines every where. I would be sorry, sir, but the fool should be as oft with your master as with my mistress: I think I saw your wisdom there.

VIOLA

Nay, an thou pass upon me, I'll no more with thee. Hold, there's expenses for thee.

CLOWN

Now Jove, in his next commodity of hair, send thee a beard!

VIOLA

By my troth, I'll tell thee, I am almost sick for one; [*Aside*] though I would not have it grow on my chin. Is thy lady within?

CLOWN

Would not a pair of these have bred, sir?

VIOLA

Yes, being kept together and put to use.

CLOWN

I would play Lord Pandarus of Phrygia, sir, to bring a Cressida to this Troilus.

VIOLA

I understand you, sir; 'tis well begged.

CLOWN

The matter, I hope, is not great, sir, begging but a beggar: Cressida was a beggar. My lady is within, sir. I will construe to them whence you come; who you are and what you would are out of my welkin, I might say 'element,' but the word is over-worn.

Exit

VIOLA

This fellow is wise enough to play the fool;
And to do that well craves a kind of wit:
He must observe their mood on whom he jests,

The quality of persons, and the time,
And, like the haggard, cheque at every feather
That comes before his eye. This is a practise
As full of labour as a wise man's art
For folly that he wisely shows is fit;
But wise men, folly-fall'n, quite taint their wit.

Enter Sir Toby Belch, and Sir Andrew

SIR TOBY BELCH

Save you, gentleman.

VIOLA

And you, sir.

SIR ANDREW

Dieu vous garde, monsieur.

VIOLA

Et vous aussi; votre serviteur.

SIR ANDREW

I hope, sir, you are; and I am yours.

SIR TOBY BELCH

Will you encounter the house? My niece is desirous you should enter, if your trade be to her.

VIOLA

I am bound to your niece, sir; I mean, she is the list of my voyage.

SIR TOBY BELCH

Taste your legs, sir; put them to motion.

VIOLA

My legs do better understand me, sir, than I understand what you mean by bidding me taste my legs.

SIR TOBY BELCH

I mean, to go, sir, to enter.

VIOLA

I will answer you with gait and entrance. But we are prevented.

Enter Olivia and Maria

Most excellent accomplished lady, the heavens rain odours on you!

SIR ANDREW

That youth's a rare courtier: 'Rain odours;' well.

VIOLA

My matter hath no voice, to your own most pregnant and vouchsafed ear.

SIR ANDREW

'Odours,' 'pregnant' and 'vouchsafed:' I'll get 'em all three all ready.

OLIVIA

Let the garden door be shut, and leave me to my earing.

Exeunt Sir Toby Belch, Sir Andrew, and Maria

Give me your hand, sir.

VIOLA

My duty, madam, and most humble service.

OLIVIA

What is your name?

VIOLA

Cesario is your servant's name, fair princess.

OLIVIA

My servant, sir! 'Twas never merry world
Since lowly feigning was call'd compliment:
You're servant to the Count Orsino, youth.

VIOLA

And he is yours, and his must needs be yours:
Your servant's servant is your servant, madam.

OLIVIA

For him, I think not on him: for his thoughts,
Would they were blanks, rather than fill'd with me!

VIOLA

Madam, I come to whet your gentle thoughts On his behalf.

OLIVIA

O, by your leave, I pray you,
I bade you never speak again of him:

But, would you undertake another suit,
I had rather hear you to solicit that
Than music from the spheres.

VIOLA

Dear lady—

OLIVIA

Give me leave, beseech you. I did send,
After the last enchantment you did here,
A ring in chase of you: so did I abuse
Myself, my servant and, I fear me, you:
Under your hard construction must I sit,
To force that on you, in a shameful cunning,
Which you knew none of yours: what might you think?
Have you not set mine honour at the stake
And baited it with all the unmuzzled thoughts
That tyrannous heart can think? To one of your receiving
Enough is shown: a cypress, not a bosom,
Hideth my heart. So, let me hear you speak.

VIOLA

I pity you.

OLIVIA

That's a degree to love.

VIOLA

No, not a grize; for 'tis a vulgar proof,
That very oft we pity enemies.

OLIVIA

Why, then, methinks 'tis time to smile again.
O, world, how apt the poor are to be proud!
If one should be a prey, how much the better
To fall before the lion than the wolf!

Clock strikes

The clock upbraids me with the waste of time.
Be not afraid, good youth, I will not have you:
And yet, when wit and youth is come to harvest,
Your wife is like to reap a proper man:
There lies your way, due west.

VIOLA

Then westward-ho!
Grace and good disposition Attend your ladyship!
You'll nothing, madam, to my lord by me?

OLIVIA

Stay: I prithee, tell me what thou thinkest of me.

VIOLA

That you do think you are not what you are.

OLIVIA

If I think so, I think the same of you.

VIOLA

Then think you right: I am not what I am.

OLIVIA

I would you were as I would have you be!

VIOLA

Would it be better, madam, than I am?
I wish it might, for now I am your fool.

OLIVIA

O, what a deal of scorn looks beautiful
In the contempt and anger of his lip!
A murderous guilt shows not itself more soon
Than love that would seem hid: love's night is noon.
Cesario, by the roses of the spring,
By maidhood, honour, truth and every thing,
I love thee so, that, maugre all thy pride,
Nor wit nor reason can my passion hide.
Do not extort thy reasons from this clause,
For that I woo, thou therefore hast no cause,
But rather reason thus with reason fetter,
Love sought is good, but given unsought better.

VIOLA

By innocence I swear, and by my youth
I have one heart, one bosom and one truth,

And that no woman has; nor never none
Shall mistress be of it, save I alone.
And so adieu, good madam: never more
Will I my master's tears to you deplore.

OLIVIA

Yet come again; for thou perhaps mayst move
That heart, which now abhors, to like his love.

Exeunt

Scene II. Olivia's House.

Enter Sir Toby Belch, Sir Andrew, and Fabian

SIR ANDREW

No, faith, I'll not stay a jot longer.

SIR TOBY BELCH

Thy reason, dear venom, give thy reason.

FABIAN

You must needs yield your reason, Sir Andrew.

SIR ANDREW

Marry, I saw your niece do more favours to the count's serving-man than ever she bestowed upon me; I saw't i' the orchard.

SIR TOBY BELCH

Did she see thee the while, old boy? Tell me that.

SIR ANDREW

As plain as I see you now.

FABIAN

This was a great argument of love in her toward you.

SIR ANDREW

'Slight, will you make an ass o' me?

FABIAN

I will prove it legitimate, sir, upon the oaths of judgment and reason.

SIR TOBY BELCH

And they have been grand-jury-men since before Noah was a sailor.

FABIAN

She did show favour to the youth in your sight only to exasperate you, to awake your dormouse valour, to put fire in your heart and brimstone in your liver. You should then have accosted her; and with some excellent jests, fire-new from the mint, you should have banged the youth into dumbness. This was looked for at your hand, and this was balked: the double gilt of this opportunity you let time wash off, and you are now sailed into the north of my lady's opinion; where you will hang like an icicle on a Dutchman's beard, unless you do redeem it by some laudable attempt either of valour or policy.

SIR ANDREW

An't be any way, it must be with valour; for policy I hate: I had as lief be a Brownist as a politician.

SIR TOBY BELCH

Why, then, build me thy fortunes upon the basis of valour. Challenge me the count's youth to fight with him; hurt him in eleven places: my niece shall take note of it; and assure thyself, there is no love-broker in the world can more prevail in man's commendation with woman than report of valour.

FABIAN

There is no way but this, Sir Andrew.

SIR ANDREW

Will either of you bear me a challenge to him?

SIR TOBY BELCH

Go, write it in a martial hand; be curst and brief; it is no matter how witty, so it be eloquent and fun of invention: taunt him with the licence of ink: if thou thou'st him some thrice, it shall not be amiss; and as many lies as will lie in thy sheet of paper, although the sheet were big enough for the bed of Ware in England, set 'em down: go, about it. Let there be gall enough in thy ink, though thou write with a goose-pen, no matter: about it.

SIR ANDREW

Where shall I find you?

SIR TOBY BELCH

We'll call thee at the cubiculo: go.

Exit Sir Andrew

FABIAN

This is a dear manikin to you, Sir Toby.

SIR TOBY BELCH

I have been dear to him, lad, some two thousand strong, or so.

FABIAN

We shall have a rare letter from him: but you'll not deliver't?

SIR TOBY BELCH

Never trust me, then; and by all means stir on the youth to an answer. I think oxen and wainropes cannot hale them together. For Andrew, if he were opened, and you find so much blood in his liver as will clog the foot of a flea, I'll eat the rest of the anatomy.

FABIAN

And his opposite, the youth, bears in his visage no great presage of cruelty.

Enter Maria

SIR TOBY BELCH

Look, where the youngest wren of nine comes.

MARIA

If you desire the spleen, and will laugh yourself into stitches, follow me. Yond gull Malvolio is turned heathen, a very renegado; for there is no Christian, that means to be saved by believing rightly, can ever believe such impossible passages of grossness. He's in yellow stockings.

SIR TOBY BELCH

And cross-gartered?

MARIA

Most villanously; like a pedant that keeps a school i' the church. I have dogged him, like his murderer. He does obey every point of the letter that I dropped to betray him: he does smile his face into more lines than is in the new map with the augmentation of the Indies: you have not seen such a thing as 'tis. I can hardly forbear hurling things at him. I know my lady will strike him: if she do, he'll smile and take't for a great favour.

SIR TOBY BELCH

Come, bring us, bring us where he is.

Exeunt

Scene III. A Street.

Enter Sebastian and Antonio

SEBASTIAN

I would not by my will have troubled you;
But, since you make your pleasure of your pains,
I will no further chide you.

ANTONIO

I could not stay behind you: my desire,
More sharp than filed steel, did spur me forth;
And not all love to see you, though so much
As might have drawn one to a longer voyage,
But jealousy what might befall your travel,
Being skilless in these parts; which to a stranger,
Unguided and unfriended, often prove
Rough and unhospitable: my willing love,
The rather by these arguments of fear,
Set forth in your pursuit.

SEBASTIAN

My kind Antonio,
I can no other answer make but thanks,

And thanks; and ever oft good turns
Are shuffled off with such uncurrent pay:
But, were my worth as is my conscience firm,
You should find better dealing. What's to do?
Shall we go see the reliques of this town?

ANTONIO

To-morrow, sir: best first go see your lodging.

SEBASTIAN

I am not weary, and 'tis long to night:
I pray you, let us satisfy our eyes
With the memorials and the things of fame
That do renown this city.

ANTONIO

Would you'ld pardon me;
I do not without danger walk these streets:
Once, in a sea-fight, 'gainst the count his galleys
I did some service; of such note indeed,
That were I ta'en here it would scarce be answer'd.

SEBASTIAN

Belike you slew great number of his people.

ANTONIO

The offence is not of such a bloody nature;
Albeit the quality of the time and quarrel
Might well have given us bloody argument.

It might have since been answer'd in repaying
What we took from them; which, for traffic's sake,
Most of our city did: only myself stood out;
For which, if I be lapsed in this place,
I shall pay dear.

SEBASTIAN

Do not then walk too open.

ANTONIO

It doth not fit me. Hold, sir, here's my purse.
In the south suburbs, at the Elephant,
Is best to lodge: I will bespeak our diet,
Whiles you beguile the time and feed your knowledge
With viewing of the town: there shall you have me.

SEBASTIAN

Why I your purse?

ANTONIO

Haply your eye shall light upon some toy
You have desire to purchase; and your store,
I think, is not for idle markets, sir.

SEBASTIAN

I'll be your purse-bearer and leave you
For an hour.

ANTONIO

To the Elephant.

SEBASTIAN

I do remember.

Exeunt

Scene IV. Olivia's Garden.

Enter Olivia and Maria

OLIVIA

I have sent after him: he says he'll come;
How shall I feast him? What bestow of him?
For youth is bought more oft than begg'd or borrow'd.
I speak too loud.
Where is Malvolio? He is sad and civil,
And suits well for a servant with my fortunes:
Where is Malvolio?

MARIA

He's coming, madam; but in very strange manner. He is, sure, possessed, madam.

OLIVIA

Why, what's the matter? Does he rave?

MARIA

No. madam, he does nothing but smile: your

ladyship were best to have some guard about you, if he come; for, sure, the man is tainted in's wits.

OLIVIA

Go call him hither.

Exit Maria

I am as mad as he,

If sad and merry madness equal be.

Re-enter Maria, with Malvolio

How now, Malvolio!

MALVOLIO

Sweet lady, ho, ho.

OLIVIA

Smilest thou? I sent for thee upon a sad occasion.

MALVOLIO

Sad, lady! I could be sad: this does make some obstruction in the blood, this cross-gartering; but what of that? If it please the eye of one, it is with me as the very true sonnet is, 'Please one, and please all.'

OLIVIA

Why, how dost thou, man? What is the matter with thee?

MALVOLIO

Not black in my mind, though yellow in my legs. It did come to his hands, and commands shall be executed: I think we do know the sweet Roman hand.

OLIVIA

Wilt thou go to bed, Malvolio?

MALVOLIO

To bed! Ay, sweet-heart, and I'll come to thee.

OLIVIA

God comfort thee! Why dost thou smile so and kiss thy hand so oft?

MARIA

How do you, Malvolio?

MALVOLIO

At your request! Yes; nightingales answer daws.

MARIA

Why appear you with this ridiculous boldness before my lady?

MALVOLIO

'Be not afraid of greatness:' 'twas well writ.

OLIVIA

What meanest thou by that, Malvolio?

MALVOLIO

'Some are born great,'—

OLIVIA

Ha!

MALVOLIO

'Some achieve greatness,'—

OLIVIA

What sayest thou?

MALVOLIO

'And some have greatness thrust upon them.'

OLIVIA

Heaven restore thee!

MALVOLIO

'Remember who commended thy yellow stockings.'

OLIVIA

Thy yellow stockings!

MALVOLIO

'And wished to see thee cross-gartered.'

OLIVIA

Cross-gartered!

MALVOLIO

'Go to thou art made, if thou desirest to be so;'—

OLIVIA

Am I made?

MALVOLIO

'If not, let me see thee a servant still.'

OLIVIA

Why, this is very midsummer madness.

Enter Servant

SERVANT

Madam, the young gentleman of the Count Orsino's is returned: I could hardly entreat him back: he attends your ladyship's pleasure.

OLIVIA

I'll come to him.

Exit Servant

Good Maria, let this fellow be looked to. Where's my cousin Toby? Let some of my people have a special care of him: I would not have him miscarry for the half of my dowry.

Exeunt Olivia and Maria

MALVOLIO

O, ho! Do you come near me now? No worse man than Sir Toby to look to me! This concurs directly with the letter: she sends him on purpose, that I may appear stubborn to him; for she incites me to that in the letter. 'Cast thy humble slough,' says she; 'be opposite with a kinsman, surly with servants; let thy tongue tang with arguments of state; put thyself into the trick of singularity;' and consequently sets down the manner how; as, a sad face, a reverend carriage, a slow tongue, in the habit of some sir of note, and so forth. I have limed her; but it is Jove's doing, and Jove make me thankful! And when she went away now, 'Let this fellow be looked to:' fellow! Not Malvolio, nor after my degree, but fellow. Why, every thing adheres together, that no dram of a scruple, no scruple of a scruple, no obstacle, no incredulous or unsafe circumstance—What can be said? Nothing that can be can come between me and the full prospect of my hopes. Well, Jove, not I, is the doer of this, and he is to be thanked.

Re-enter Maria, with Sir Toby Belch and Fabian

SIR TOBY BELCH

Which way is he, in the name of sanctity? If all the devils of hell be drawn in little, and Legion himself possessed him, yet I'll speak to him.

FABIAN

Here he is, here he is. How is't with you, sir? How is't with you, man?

MALVOLIO

Go off; I discard you: let me enjoy my private: go off.

MARIA

Lo, how hollow the fiend speaks within him! Did not I tell you? Sir Toby, my lady prays you to have a care of him.

MALVOLIO

Ah, ha! Does she so?

SIR TOBY BELCH

Go to, go to; peace, peace; we must deal gently with him: let me alone. How do you, Malvolio? How is't with you? What, man! Defy the devil: consider, he's an enemy to mankind.

MALVOLIO

Do you know what you say?

MARIA

La you, an you speak ill of the devil, how he takes it at heart! Pray God, he be not bewitched!

FABIAN

Carry his water to the wise woman.

MARIA

Marry, and it shall be done to-morrow morning, if I live. My lady would not lose him for more than I'll say.

MALVOLIO

How now, mistress!

MARIA

O Lord!

SIR TOBY BELCH

Prithee, hold thy peace; this is not the way: do you not see you move him? Let me alone with him.

FABIAN

No way but gentleness; gently, gently: the fiend is rough, and will not be roughly used.

SIR TOBY BELCH

Why, how now, my bawcock! How dost thou, chuck?

MALVOLIO

Sir!

SIR TOBY BELCH

Ay, Biddy, come with me. What, man! 'Tis not for gravity to play at cherry-pit with Satan: hang him, foul collier!

MARIA

Get him to say his prayers, good Sir Toby, get him to pray.

MALVOLIO

My prayers, minx!

MARIA

No, I warrant you, he will not hear of godliness.

MALVOLIO

Go, hang yourselves all! You are idle shallow things: I am not of your element: you shall know more hereafter.

Exit

SIR TOBY BELCH

Is't possible?

FABIAN

If this were played upon a stage now, I could condemn it as an improbable fiction.

SIR TOBY BELCH

His very genius hath taken the infection of the device, man.

MARIA

Nay, pursue him now, lest the device take air and taint.

FABIAN

Why, we shall make him mad indeed.

MARIA

The house will be the quieter.

SIR TOBY BELCH

Come, we'll have him in a dark room and bound. My niece is already in the belief that he's mad: we may carry it thus, for our pleasure and his penance, till our very pastime, tired out of breath, prompt us to have mercy on him: at which time we will bring the device to the bar and crown thee for a finder of madmen. But see, but see.

Enter Sir Andrew

FABIAN

More matter for a May morning.

SIR ANDREW

Here's the challenge, read it: warrant there's vinegar and pepper in't.

FABIAN

Is't so saucy?

SIR ANDREW

Ay, is't, I warrant him: do but read.

SIR TOBY BELCH

Give me.

[Reads] *'Youth, whatsoever thou art, thou art but a scurvy fellow.'*

FABIAN

Good, and valiant.

SIR TOBY BELCH

[Reads] *'Wonder not, nor admire not in thy mind, why I do call thee so, for I will show thee no reason for't.'*

FABIAN

A good note; that keeps you from the blow of the law.

SIR TOBY BELCH

[Reads] *'Thou comest to the lady Olivia, and in my sight she uses thee kindly: but thou liest in thy throat; that is not the matter I challenge thee for.'*

FABIAN

Very brief, and to exceeding good sense—less.

SIR TOBY BELCH

[*Reads*] *'I will waylay thee going home; where if it be thy chance to kill me,'*—

FABIAN

Good.

SIR TOBY BELCH

[*Reads*] *'Thou killest me like a rogue and a villain.'*

FABIAN

Still you keep o' the windy side of the law: good.

SIR TOBY BELCH

[*Reads*] *'Fare thee well; and God have mercy upon one of our souls! He may have mercy upon mine; but my hope is better, and so look to thyself. Thy friend, as thou usest him, and thy sworn enemy,*

Andrew Aguecheek.

If this letter move him not, his legs cannot: I'll give't him.

MARIA

You may have very fit occasion for't: he is now in some commerce with my lady, and will by and by depart.

SIR TOBY BELCH

Go, Sir Andrew: scout me for him at the corner the orchard like a bum-baily: so soon as ever thou seest him, draw; and, as thou drawest swear horrible; for it comes to pass oft that a terrible oath, with a swaggering accent sharply twanged off, gives manhood more approbation than ever proof itself would have earned him. Away!

SIR ANDREW

Nay, let me alone for swearing.

Exit

SIR TOBY BELCH

Now will not I deliver his letter: for the behavior of the young gentleman gives him out to be of good capacity and breeding; his employment between his lord and my niece confirms no less: therefore this letter, being so excellently ignorant, will breed no terror in the youth: he will find it comes from a clodpole. But, sir, I will deliver his challenge by word of mouth; set upon Aguecheek a notable report of valour; and drive the gentleman, as I know his youth will aptly receive it, into a most hideous opinion of his rage, skill, fury and impetuosity. This will so fright them both that they will kill one another by the look, like cockatrices.

Re-enter Olivia, with Viola

FABIAN

Here he comes with your niece: give them way till he take leave, and presently after him.

SIR TOBY BELCH

I will meditate the while upon some horrid message for a challenge.

Exeunt Sir Toby Belch, Fabian, and Maria

OLIVIA

I have said too much unto a heart of stone
And laid mine honour too unchary out:
There's something in me that reproves my fault;
But such a headstrong potent fault it is,
That it but mocks reproof.

VIOLA

With the same 'havior that your passion bears
Goes on my master's grief.

OLIVIA

Here, wear this jewel for me, 'tis my picture;
Refuse it not; it hath no tongue to vex you;
And I beseech you come again to-morrow.
What shall you ask of me that I'll deny,
That honour saved may upon asking give?

VIOLA

Nothing but this; your true love for my master.

OLIVIA

How with mine honour may I give him that
Which I have given to you?

VIOLA

I will acquit you.

OLIVIA

Well, come again to-morrow: fare thee well:
A fiend like thee might bear my soul to hell.

Exit

Re-enter Sir Toby Belch and Fabian

SIR TOBY BELCH

Gentleman, God save thee.

VIOLA

And you, sir.

SIR TOBY BELCH

That defence thou hast, betake thee to't: of what nature the wrongs are thou hast done him, I know not; but thy intercepter, full of despite, bloody as the hunter, attends thee at the orchard-end: dismount thy tuck, be yare in thy preparation, for thy assailant is quick, skilful and deadly.

VIOLA

You mistake, sir; I am sure no man hath any quarrel to me: my remembrance is very free and clear from any image of offence done to any man.

SIR TOBY BELCH

You'll find it otherwise, I assure you: therefore, if you hold your life at any price, betake you to your guard; for your opposite hath in him what youth, strength, skill and wrath can furnish man withal.

VIOLA

I pray you, sir, what is he?

SIR TOBY BELCH

He is knight, dubbed with unhatched rapier and on carpet consideration; but he is a devil in private brawl: souls and bodies hath he divorced three; and his incensement at this moment is so implacable, that satisfaction can be none but by pangs of death and sepulchre. Hob, nob, is his word; give't or take't.

VIOLA

I will return again into the house and desire some conduct of the lady. I am no fighter. I have heard of some kind of men that put quarrels purposely on others, to taste their valour: belike this is a man of that quirk.

SIR TOBY BELCH

Sir, no; his indignation derives itself out of a very competent injury: therefore, get you on and give him his desire. Back you shall not to the house, unless you undertake that with me which with as much safety you might answer him: therefore, on, or strip your sword stark naked; for meddle you must, that's certain, or forswear to wear iron about you.

VIOLA

This is as uncivil as strange. I beseech you, do me this courteous office, as to know of the knight what my offence to him is: it is something of my negligence, nothing of my purpose.

SIR TOBY BELCH

I will do so. Signior Fabian, stay you by this gentleman till my return.

Exit

VIOLA

Pray you, sir, do you know of this matter?

FABIAN

I know the knight is incensed against you, even to a mortal arbitrement; but nothing of the circumstance more.

VIOLA

I beseech you, what manner of man is he?

FABIAN

Nothing of that wonderful promise, to read him by his form, as you are like to find him in the proof of his valour. He is, indeed, sir, the most skilful, bloody and fatal opposite that you could possibly have found in any part of Illyria. Will you walk towards him? I will make your peace with him if I can.

VIOLA

I shall be much bound to you for't: I am one that had rather go with sir priest than sir knight: I care not who knows so much of my mettle.

Exeunt

Re-enter Sir Toby Belch, with Sir Andrew

SIR TOBY BELCH

Why, man, he's a very devil; I have not seen such a firago. I had a pass with him, rapier, scabbard and all, and he gives me the stuck in with such a mortal motion, that it is inevitable; and on the answer, he pays you as surely as your feet hit the ground they step on. They say he has been fencer to the Sophy.

SIR ANDREW

Pox on't, I'll not meddle with him.

SIR TOBY BELCH

Ay, but he will not now be pacified: Fabian can scarce hold him yonder.

SIR ANDREW

Plague on't, an I thought he had been valiant and so cunning in fence, I'ld have seen him damned ere I'ld have challenged him. Let him let the matter slip, and I'll give him my horse, grey Capilet.

SIR TOBY BELCH

I'll make the motion: stand here, make a good show on't: this shall end without the perdition of souls. [*Aside*] Marry, I'll ride your horse as well as I ride you.

Re-enter Fabian and Viola

[*To Fabian*] I have his horse to take up the quarrel: I have persuaded him the youth's a devil.

FABIAN

He is as horribly conceited of him; and pants and looks pale, as if a bear were at his heels.

SIR TOBY BELCH

[*To Viola*] There's no remedy, sir; he will fight with you for's oath sake: marry, he hath better bethought him of his quarrel, and he finds that now scarce to be worth talking of: therefore draw, for the supportance of his vow; he protests he will not hurt you.

VIOLA

[*Aside*] Pray God defend me! A little thing would make me tell them how much I lack of a man.

FABIAN

Give ground, if you see him furious.

SIR TOBY BELCH

Come, Sir Andrew, there's no remedy; the gentleman will, for his honour's sake, have one bout with you; he cannot by the duello avoid it: but he has promised me, as he is a gentleman and a soldier, he will not hurt you. Come on; to't.

SIR ANDREW

Pray God, he keep his oath!

VIOLA

I do assure you, 'tis against my will.

They draw

Enter Antonio

ANTONIO

Put up your sword. If this young gentleman
Have done offence, I take the fault on me:
If you offend him, I for him defy you.

SIR TOBY BELCH

You, sir! Why, what are you?

ANTONIO

One, sir, that for his love dares yet do more

Than you have heard him brag to you he will.

SIR TOBY BELCH

Nay, if you be an undertaker, I am for you.

They draw

Enter Officers

FABIAN

O good Sir Toby, hold! Here come the officers.

SIR TOBY BELCH

I'll be with you anon.

VIOLA

Pray, sir, put your sword up, if you please.

SIR ANDREW

Marry, will I, sir; and, for that I promised you, I'll be as good as my word: he will bear you easily and reins well.

FIRST OFFICER

This is the man; do thy office.

SECOND OFFICER

Antonio, I arrest thee at the suit of Count Orsino.

ANTONIO

You do mistake me, sir.

FIRST OFFICER

No, sir, no jot; I know your favour well,
Though now you have no sea-cap on your head.
Take him away: he knows I know him well.

ANTONIO

I must obey.
[*To Viola*] This comes with seeking you:
But there's no remedy; I shall answer it.
What will you do, now my necessity
Makes me to ask you for my purse? It grieves me
Much more for what I cannot do for you
Than what befalls myself. You stand amazed;
But be of comfort.

SECOND OFFICER

Come, sir, away.

ANTONIO

I must entreat of you some of that money.

VIOLA

What money, sir?
For the fair kindness you have show'd me here,
And, part, being prompted by your present trouble,
Out of my lean and low ability
I'll lend you something: my having is not much;

I'll make division of my present with you:
Hold, there's half my coffer.

ANTONIO

Will you deny me now?
Is't possible that my deserts to you
Can lack persuasion? Do not tempt my misery,
Lest that it make me so unsound a man
As to upbraid you with those kindnesses
That I have done for you.

VIOLA

I know of none;
Nor know I you by voice or any feature:
I hate ingratitude more in a man
Than lying, vainness, babbling, drunkenness,
Or any taint of vice whose strong corruption
Inhabits our frail blood.

ANTONIO

O heavens themselves!

SECOND OFFICER

Come, sir, I pray you, go.

ANTONIO

Let me speak a little. This youth that you see here
I snatch'd one half out of the jaws of death,
Relieved him with such sanctity of love,

And to his image, which methought did promise
Most venerable worth, did I devotion.

FIRST OFFICER

What's that to us? The time goes by: away!

ANTONIO

But O how vile an idol proves this god
Thou hast, Sebastian, done good feature shame.
In nature there's no blemish but the mind;
None can be call'd deform'd but the unkind:
Virtue is beauty, but the beauteous evil
Are empty trunks o'erflourish'd by the devil.

FIRST OFFICER

The man grows mad: away with him! Come, come, sir.

ANTONIO

Lead me on.

Exit with Officers

VIOLA

Methinks his words do from such passion fly,
That he believes himself: so do not I.
Prove true, imagination, O, prove true,
That I, dear brother, be now ta'en for you!

SIR TOBY BELCH

Come hither, knight; come hither, Fabian: we'll whisper o'er a couplet or two of most sage saws.

VIOLA

He named Sebastian: I my brother know
Yet living in my glass; even such and so
In favour was my brother, and he went
Still in this fashion, colour, ornament,
For him I imitate: O, if it prove,
Tempests are kind and salt waves fresh in love.

Exit

SIR TOBY BELCH

A very dishonest paltry boy, and more a coward than a hare: his dishonesty appears in leaving his friend here in necessity and denying him; and for his cowardship, ask Fabian.

FABIAN

A coward, a most devout coward, religious in it.

SIR ANDREW

'Slid, I'll after him again and beat him.

SIR TOBY BELCH

Do; cuff him soundly, but never draw thy sword.

SIR ANDREW

An I do not—

Exit

FABIAN

Come, let's see the event.

SIR TOBY BELCH

I dare lay any money 'twill be nothing yet.

Exeunt

***

ACT IV

Scene I. Before Olivia's House.

Enter Sebastian and Clown

CLOWN

Will you make me believe that I am not sent for you?

SEBASTIAN

Go to, go to, thou art a foolish fellow: Let me be clear of thee.

CLOWN

Well held out, i' faith! No, I do not know you; nor I am not sent to you by my lady, to bid you come speak with her; nor your name is not Master Cesario; nor this is not my nose neither. Nothing that is so is so.

SEBASTIAN

I prithee, vent thy folly somewhere else: Thou know'st not me.

CLOWN

Vent my folly! He has heard that word of some great man and now applies it to a fool. Vent my folly! I am afraid this great lubber, the world, will prove a cockney. I prithee now, ungird thy strangeness and tell me what I shall vent to my lady: shall I vent to her that thou art coming?

SEBASTIAN

I prithee, foolish Greek, depart from me: There's money for thee: if you tarry longer, I shall give worse payment.

CLOWN

By my troth, thou hast an open hand. These wise men that give fools money get themselves a good report—after fourteen years' purchase.

Enter Sir Andrew, Sir Toby Belch, and Fabian

SIR ANDREW

Now, sir, have I met you again? There's for you.

SEBASTIAN

Why, there's for thee, and there, and there. Are all the people mad?

SIR TOBY BELCH

Hold, sir, or I'll throw your dagger o'er the house.

CLOWN

This will I tell my lady straight: I would not be in some of your coats for two pence.

Exit

SIR TOBY BELCH

Come on, sir; hold.

SIR ANDREW

Nay, let him alone: I'll go another way to work with

him; I'll have an action of battery against him, if there be any law in Illyria: though I struck him first, yet it's no matter for that.

SEBASTIAN

Let go thy hand.

SIR TOBY BELCH

Come, sir, I will not let you go. Come, my young soldier, put up your iron: you are well fleshed; come on.

SEBASTIAN

I will be free from thee. What wouldst thou now? If thou darest tempt me further, draw thy sword.

SIR TOBY BELCH

What, what? Nay, then I must have an ounce or two of this malapert blood from you.

Enter Olivia

OLIVIA

Hold, Toby; on thy life I charge thee, hold!

SIR TOBY BELCH

Madam!

OLIVIA

Will it be ever thus? Ungracious wretch,
Fit for the mountains and the barbarous caves,
Where manners ne'er were preach'd! Out of my sight!

Be not offended, dear Cesario.
Rudesby, be gone!

Exeunt Sir Toby Belch, Sir Andrew, and Fabian

I prithee, gentle friend,
Let thy fair wisdom, not thy passion, sway
In this uncivil and thou unjust extent
Against thy peace. Go with me to my house,
And hear thou there how many fruitless pranks
This ruffian hath botch'd up, that thou thereby
Mayst smile at this: thou shalt not choose but go:
Do not deny. Beshrew his soul for me,
He started one poor heart of mine in thee.

SEBASTIAN

What relish is in this? How runs the stream?
Or I am mad, or else this is a dream:
Let fancy still my sense in Lethe steep;
If it be thus to dream, still let me sleep!

OLIVIA

Nay, come, I prithee; would thou'ldst be ruled by me!

SEBASTIAN

Madam, I will.

OLIVIA

O, say so, and so be!

Exeunt

Scene II. Olivia's House.

Enter Maria and Clown

MARIA

Nay, I prithee, put on this gown and this beard; make him believe thou art Sir Topas the curate: do it quickly; I'll call Sir Toby the whilst.

Exit

CLOWN

Well, I'll put it on, and I will dissemble myself in't; and I would I were the first that ever dissembled in such a gown. I am not tall enough to become the function well, nor lean enough to be thought a good student; but to be said an honest man and a good housekeeper goes as fairly as to say a careful man and a great scholar. The competitors enter.

Enter Sir Toby Belch and Maria

SIR TOBY BELCH

Jove bless thee, master Parson.

CLOWN

Bonos dies, Sir Toby: for, as the old hermit of Prague, that never saw pen and ink, very wittily said to a niece of King Gorboduc, 'That that is is;' so I, being Master Parson, am Master Parson; for, what is 'that' but 'that,' and 'is' but 'is'?

SIR TOBY BELCH

To him, Sir Topas.

CLOWN

What, ho, I say! Peace in this prison!

SIR TOBY BELCH

The knave counterfeits well; a good knave.

MALVOLIO

[*Within*] Who calls there?

CLOWN

Sir Topas the curate, who comes to visit Malvolio the lunatic.

MALVOLIO

Sir Topas, Sir Topas, good Sir Topas, go to my lady.

CLOWN

Out, hyperbolical fiend! How vexest thou this man! Talkest thou nothing but of ladies?

SIR TOBY BELCH

Well said, Master Parson.

MALVOLIO

Sir Topas, never was man thus wronged: good Sir Topas, do not think I am mad: they have laid me here in hideous darkness.

CLOWN

Fie, thou dishonest Satan! I call thee by the most

modest terms; for I am one of those gentle ones that will use the devil himself with courtesy: sayest thou that house is dark?

MALVOLIO

As hell, Sir Topas.

CLOWN

Why it hath bay windows transparent as barricadoes, and the clearstores toward the south north are as lustrous as ebony; and yet complainest thou of obstruction?

MALVOLIO

I am not mad, Sir Topas: I say to you, this house is dark.

CLOWN

Madman, thou errest: I say, there is no darkness but ignorance; in which thou art more puzzled than the Egyptians in their fog.

MALVOLIO

I say, this house is as dark as ignorance, though ignorance were as dark as hell; and I say, there was never man thus abused. I am no more mad than you are: make the trial of it in any constant question.

CLOWN

What is the opinion of Pythagoras concerning wild fowl?

MALVOLIO

That the soul of our grandam might haply inhabit a bird.

CLOWN

What thinkest thou of his opinion?

MALVOLIO

I think nobly of the soul, and no way approve his opinion.

CLOWN

Fare thee well. Remain thou still in darkness: thou shalt hold the opinion of Pythagoras ere I will allow of thy wits, and fear to kill a woodcock, lest thou dispossess the soul of thy grandam. Fare thee well.

MALVOLIO

Sir Topas, Sir Topas!

SIR TOBY BELCH

My most exquisite Sir Topas!

CLOWN

Nay, I am for all waters.

MARIA

Thou mightst have done this without thy beard and gown: he sees thee not.

SIR TOBY BELCH

To him in thine own voice, and bring me word how thou findest him: I would we were well rid of this knavery. If he may be conveniently delivered, I would he were, for I am now so far in offence with my niece that I cannot pursue with any safety this sport to the upshot. Come by and by to my chamber.

Exeunt Sir Toby Belch and Maria

CLOWN

[*Singing*] 'Hey, Robin, jolly Robin,
Tell me how thy lady does.'

MALVOLIO

Fool!

CLOWN

'My lady is unkind, perdy.'

MALVOLIO

Fool!

CLOWN

'Alas, why is she so?'

MALVOLIO

Fool, I say!

CLOWN

'She loves another'—Who calls, ha?

MALVOLIO

Good fool, as ever thou wilt deserve well at my hand, help me to a candle, and pen, ink and paper: as I am a gentleman, I will live to be thankful to thee for't.

CLOWN

Master Malvolio?

MALVOLIO

Ay, good fool.

CLOWN

Alas, sir, how fell you besides your five wits?

MALVOLIO

Fool, there was never a man so notoriously abused: I am as well in my wits, fool, as thou art.

CLOWN

But as well? Then you are mad indeed, if you be no better in your wits than a fool.

MALVOLIO

They have here propertied me; keep me in darkness, send ministers to me, asses, and do all they can to face me out of my wits.

CLOWN

Advise you what you say; the minister is here. Malvolio, Malvolio, thy wits the heavens restore! Endeavour thyself to sleep, and leave thy vain bibble babble.

MALVOLIO

Sir Topas!

CLOWN

Maintain no words with him, good fellow. Who, I, sir? Not I, sir. God be wi' you, good Sir Topas. Merry, amen. I will, sir, I will.

MALVOLIO

Fool, fool, fool, I say!

CLOWN

Alas, sir, be patient. What say you sir? I am shent for speaking to you.

MALVOLIO

Good fool, help me to some light and some paper: I tell thee, I am as well in my wits as any man in Illyria.

CLOWN

Well-a-day that you were, sir

MALVOLIO

By this hand, I am. Good fool, some ink, paper and

light; and convey what I will set down to my lady: it shall advantage thee more than ever the bearing of letter did.

CLOWN

I will help you to't. But tell me true, are you not mad indeed? Or do you but counterfeit?

MALVOLIO

Believe me, I am not; I tell thee true.

CLOWN

Nay, I'll ne'er believe a madman till I see his brains. I will fetch you light and paper and ink.

MALVOLIO

Fool, I'll requite it in the highest degree: I prithee, be gone.

CLOWN

[*Singing*] I am gone, sir,
And anon, sir,
I'll be with you again,
In a trice,
Like to the old Vice,
Your need to sustain;
Who, with dagger of lath,
In his rage and his wrath,
Cries, ah, ha! To the devil:

Like a mad lad, Pare thy nails, dad;
Adieu, good man devil.

Exit

Scene III. Olivia's Garden.

Enter Sebastian

SEBASTIAN

This is the air; that is the glorious sun;
This pearl she gave me, I do feel't and see't;
And though 'tis wonder that enwraps me thus,
Yet 'tis not madness. Where's Antonio, then?
I could not find him at the Elephant:
Yet there he was; and there I found this credit,
That he did range the town to seek me out.
His counsel now might do me golden service;
For though my soul disputes well with my sense,
That this may be some error, but no madness,
Yet doth this accident and flood of fortune
So far exceed all instance, all discourse,
That I am ready to distrust mine eyes
And wrangle with my reason that persuades me
To any other trust but that I am mad
Or else the lady's mad; yet, if 'twere so,
She could not sway her house, command her followers,

Take and give back affairs and their dispatch
With such a smooth, discreet and stable bearing
As I perceive she does: there's something in't
That is deceiveable. But here the lady comes.

Enter Olivia and Priest

OLIVIA

Blame not this haste of mine. If you mean well,
Now go with me and with this holy man
Into the chantry by: there, before him,
And underneath that consecrated roof,
Plight me the full assurance of your faith;
That my most jealous and too doubtful soul
May live at peace. He shall conceal it
Whiles you are willing it shall come to note,
What time we will our celebration keep
According to my birth. What do you say?

SEBASTIAN

I'll follow this good man, and go with you;
And, having sworn truth, ever will be true.

OLIVIA

Then lead the way, good father; and heavens so shine,
That they may fairly note this act of mine!

Exeunt

***

ACT V

Scene I. Before Olivia's House.

Enter Clown and Fabian

FABIAN

Now, as thou lovest me, let me see his letter.

CLOWN

Good Master Fabian, grant me another request.

FABIAN

Any thing.

CLOWN

Do not desire to see this letter.

FABIAN

This is, to give a dog, and in recompense desire my dog again.

Enter Duke Orsino, Viola, Curio, and Lords

DUKE ORSINO

Belong you to the Lady Olivia, friends?

CLOWN

Ay, sir; we are some of her trappings.

DUKE ORSINO

I know thee well; how dost thou, my good fellow?

CLOWN

Truly, sir, the better for my foes and the worse for my friends.

DUKE ORSINO

Just the contrary; the better for thy friends.

CLOWN

No, sir, the worse.

DUKE ORSINO

How can that be?

CLOWN

Marry, sir, they praise me and make an ass of me; now my foes tell me plainly I am an ass: so that by my foes, sir I profit in the knowledge of myself, and by my friends, I am abused: so that, conclusions to be as kisses, if your four negatives make your two affirmatives why then, the worse for my friends and the better for my foes.

DUKE ORSINO

Why, this is excellent.

CLOWN

By my troth, sir, no; though it please you to be one of my friends.

DUKE ORSINO

Thou shalt not be the worse for me: there's gold.

CLOWN

But that it would be double-dealing, sir, I would you could make it another.

DUKE ORSINO

O, you give me ill counsel.

CLOWN

Put your grace in your pocket, sir, for this once, and let your flesh and blood obey it.

DUKE ORSINO

Well, I will be so much a sinner, to be a double-dealer: there's another.

CLOWN

Primo, secundo, tertio, is a good play; and the old saying is, the third pays for all: the triplex, sir, is a good tripping measure; or the bells of Saint Bennet, sir, may put you in mind; one, two, three.

DUKE ORSINO

You can fool no more money out of me at this throw: if you will let your lady know I am here to speak with her, and bring her along with you, it may awake my bounty further.

CLOWN

Marry, sir, lullaby to your bounty till I come again. I go, sir; but I would not have you to think that my desire of having is the sin of covetousness: but, as you say, sir, let your bounty take a nap, I will awake it anon.

Exit

VIOLA

Here comes the man, sir, that did rescue me.

Enter Antonio and Officers

DUKE ORSINO

That face of his I do remember well;
Yet, when I saw it last, it was besmear'd
As black as Vulcan in the smoke of war:
A bawbling vessel was he captain of,
For shallow draught and bulk unprizable;
With which such scathful grapple did he make
With the most noble bottom of our fleet,
That very envy and the tongue of loss
Cried fame and honour on him. What's the matter?

FIRST OFFICER

Orsino, this is that Antonio
That took the *Phoenix* and her fraught from Candy;

And this is he that did the *Tiger* board,
When your young nephew Titus lost his leg:
Here in the streets, desperate of shame and state,
In private brabble did we apprehend him.

VIOLA

He did me kindness, sir, drew on my side;
But in conclusion put strange speech upon me:
I know not what 'twas but distraction.

DUKE ORSINO

Notable pirate! Thou salt-water thief!
What foolish boldness brought thee to their mercies,
Whom thou, in terms so bloody and so dear,
Hast made thine enemies?

ANTONIO

Orsino, noble sir,
Be pleased that I shake off these names you give me:
Antonio never yet was thief or pirate,
Though I confess, on base and ground enough,
Orsino's enemy. A witchcraft drew me hither:
That most ingrateful boy there by your side,
From the rude sea's enraged and foamy mouth
Did I redeem; a wreck past hope he was:
His life I gave him and did thereto add

My love, without retention or restraint,
All his in dedication; for his sake
Did I expose myself, pure for his love,
Into the danger of this adverse town;
Drew to defend him when he was beset:
Where being apprehended, his false cunning,
Not meaning to partake with me in danger,
Taught him to face me out of his acquaintance,
And grew a twenty years removed thing
While one would wink; denied me mine own purse,
Which I had recommended to his use
Not half an hour before.

VIOLA

How can this be?

DUKE ORSINO

When came he to this town?

ANTONIO

To-day, my lord; and for three months before,
No interim, not a minute's vacancy,
Both day and night did we keep company.

Enter Olivia and Attendants

DUKE ORSINO

Here comes the countess: now heaven walks on earth.
But for thee, fellow; fellow, thy words are madness:

Three months this youth hath tended upon me;

But more of that anon. Take him aside.

OLIVIA

What would my lord, but that he may not have,

Wherein Olivia may seem serviceable?

Cesario, you do not keep promise with me.

VIOLA

Madam!

DUKE ORSINO

Gracious Olivia—

OLIVIA

What do you say, Cesario? Good my lord—

VIOLA

My lord would speak; my duty hushes me.

OLIVIA

If it be aught to the old tune, my lord,

It is as fat and fulsome to mine ear

As howling after music.

DUKE ORSINO

Still so cruel?

OLIVIA

Still so constant, lord.

DUKE ORSINO

What, to perverseness? You uncivil lady,

To whose ingrate and unauspicious altars
My soul the faithfull'st offerings hath breathed out
That e'er devotion tender'd! What shall I do?

OLIVIA

Even what it please my lord, that shall become
him.

DUKE ORSINO

Why should I not, had I the heart to do it,
Like to the Egyptian thief at point of death,
Kill what I love?—a savage jealousy
That sometimes savours nobly. But hear me this:
Since you to non-regardance cast my faith,
And that I partly know the instrument
That screws me from my true place in your favour,
Live you the marble-breasted tyrant still;
But this your minion, whom I know you love,
And whom, by heaven I swear, I tender dearly,
Him will I tear out of that cruel eye,
Where he sits crowned in his master's spite.
Come, boy, with me; my thoughts are ripe in
mischief:
I'll sacrifice the lamb that I do love,
To spite a raven's heart within a dove.

VIOLA

And I, most jocund, apt and willingly,
To do you rest, a thousand deaths would die.

OLIVIA

Where goes Cesario?

VIOLA

After him I love
More than I love these eyes, more than my life,
More, by all mores, than e'er I shall love wife.
If I do feign, you witnesses above
Punish my life for tainting of my love!

OLIVIA

Ay me, detested! How am I beguiled!

VIOLA

Who does beguile you? Who does do you wrong?

OLIVIA

Hast thou forgot thyself? Is it so long?
Call forth the holy father.

DUKE ORSINO

Come, away!

OLIVIA

Whither, my lord? Cesario, husband, stay.

DUKE ORSINO

Husband!

OLIVIA

Ay, husband: can he that deny?

DUKE ORSINO

Her husband, sirrah!

VIOLA

No, my lord, not I.

OLIVIA

Alas, it is the baseness of thy fear
That makes thee strangle thy propriety:
Fear not, Cesario; take thy fortunes up;
Be that thou know'st thou art, and then thou art
As great as that thou fear'st.

Enter Priest

O, welcome, father!
Father, I charge thee, by thy reverence,
Here to unfold, though lately we intended
To keep in darkness what occasion now
Reveals before 'tis ripe, what thou dost know
Hath newly pass'd between this youth and me.

PRIEST

A contract of eternal bond of love,
Confirm'd by mutual joinder of your hands,
Attested by the holy close of lips,
Strengthen'd by interchangement of your rings;

And all the ceremony of this compact
Seal'd in my function, by my testimony:
Since when, my watch hath told me, toward my grave
I have travell'd but two hours.

DUKE ORSINO

O thou dissembling cub! What wilt thou be
When time hath sow'd a grizzle on thy case?
Or will not else thy craft so quickly grow,
That thine own trip shall be thine overthrow?
Farewell, and take her; but direct thy feet
Where thou and I henceforth may never meet.

VIOLA

My lord, I do protest—

OLIVIA

O, do not swear!
Hold little faith, though thou hast too much fear.

Enter Sir Andrew

SIR ANDREW

For the love of God, a surgeon! Send one presently to Sir Toby.

OLIVIA

What's the matter?

SIR ANDREW

He has broke my head across and has given Sir Toby

a bloody coxcomb too: for the love of God, your help! I had rather than forty pound I were at home.

OLIVIA

Who has done this, Sir Andrew?

SIR ANDREW

The count's gentleman, one Cesario: we took him for a coward, but he's the very devil incardinate.

DUKE ORSINO

My gentleman, Cesario?

SIR ANDREW

'Od's lifelings, here he is! You broke my head for nothing; and that that I did, I was set on to do't by Sir Toby.

VIOLA

Why do you speak to me? I never hurt you:
You drew your sword upon me without cause;
But I bespoke you fair, and hurt you not.

SIR ANDREW

If a bloody coxcomb be a hurt, you have hurt me: I think you set nothing by a bloody coxcomb.

Enter Sir Toby Belch and Clown

Here comes Sir Toby halting; you shall hear more: but if he had not been in drink, he would have tickled you othergates than he did.

DUKE ORSINO

How now, gentleman! How is't with you?

SIR TOBY BELCH

That's all one: has hurt me, and there's the end on't. Sot, didst see Dick surgeon, sot?

CLOWN

O, he's drunk, Sir Toby, an hour agone; his eyes were set at eight i' the morning.

SIR TOBY BELCH

Then he's a rogue, and a passy measures panyn: I hate a drunken rogue.

OLIVIA

Away with him! Who hath made this havoc with them?

SIR ANDREW

I'll help you, Sir Toby, because we'll be dressed together.

SIR TOBY BELCH

Will you help? An ass-head and a coxcomb and a knave, a thin-faced knave, a gull!

OLIVIA

Get him to bed, and let his hurt be look'd to.

Exeunt Clown, Fabian, Sir Toby Belch, and Sir Andrew

Enter Sebastian

SEBASTIAN

I am sorry, madam, I have hurt your kinsman:
But, had it been the brother of my blood,
I must have done no less with wit and safety.
You throw a strange regard upon me, and by that
I do perceive it hath offended you:
Pardon me, sweet one, even for the vows
We made each other but so late ago.

DUKE ORSINO

One face, one voice, one habit, and two persons,
A natural perspective, that is and is not!

SEBASTIAN

Antonio, O my dear Antonio!
How have the hours rack'd and tortured me,
Since I have lost thee!

ANTONIO

Sebastian are you?

SEBASTIAN

Fear'st thou that, Antonio?

ANTONIO

How have you made division of yourself?
An apple, cleft in two, is not more twin
Than these two creatures. Which is Sebastian?

OLIVIA

Most wonderful!

SEBASTIAN

Do I stand there? I never had a brother;
Nor can there be that deity in my nature,
Of here and every where. I had a sister,
Whom the blind waves and surges have devour'd.
Of charity, what kin are you to me?
What countryman? What name? What parentage?

VIOLA

Of Messaline: Sebastian was my father;
Such a Sebastian was my brother too,
So went he suited to his watery tomb:
If spirits can assume both form and suit
You come to fright us.

SEBASTIAN

A spirit I am indeed;
But am in that dimension grossly clad
Which from the womb I did participate.
Were you a woman, as the rest goes even,
I should my tears let fall upon your cheek,
And say 'Thrice-welcome, drowned Viola!'

VIOLA

My father had a mole upon his brow.

SEBASTIAN

And so had mine.

VIOLA

And died that day when Viola from her birth
Had number'd thirteen years.

SEBASTIAN

O, that record is lively in my soul!
He finished indeed his mortal act
That day that made my sister thirteen years.

VIOLA

If nothing lets to make us happy both
But this my masculine usurp'd attire,
Do not embrace me till each circumstance
Of place, time, fortune, do cohere and jump
That I am Viola: which to confirm,
I'll bring you to a captain in this town,
Where lie my maiden weeds; by whose gentle help
I was preserved to serve this noble count.
All the occurrence of my fortune since
Hath been between this lady and this lord.

SEBASTIAN

[*To Olivia*] So comes it, lady, you have been mistook:
But nature to her bias drew in that.
You would have been contracted to a maid;

Nor are you therein, by my life, deceived,
You are betroth'd both to a maid and man.

DUKE ORSINO

Be not amazed; right noble is his blood.
If this be so, as yet the glass seems true,
I shall have share in this most happy wreck.
[*To Viola*] Boy, thou hast said to me a thousand times
Thou never shouldst love woman like to me.

VIOLA

And all those sayings will I overswear;
And those swearings keep as true in soul
As doth that orbed continent the fire
That severs day from night.

DUKE ORSINO

Give me thy hand;
And let me see thee in thy woman's weeds.

VIOLA

The captain that did bring me first on shore
Hath my maid's garments: he upon some action
Is now in durance, at Malvolio's suit,
A gentleman, and follower of my lady's.

OLIVIA

He shall enlarge him: fetch Malvolio hither:

And yet, alas, now I remember me,
They say, poor gentleman, he's much distract.

Re-enter Clown with a letter, and Fabian

A most extracting frenzy of mine own
From my remembrance clearly banish'd his.
How does he, sirrah?

CLOWN

Truly, madam, he holds Belzebub at the staves's end as well as a man in his case may do: has here writ a letter to you; I should have given't you to-day morning, but as a madman's epistles are no gospels, so it skills not much when they are delivered.

OLIVIA

Open't, and read it.

CLOWN

Look then to be well edified when the fool delivers the madman. [*Reads*] '*By the Lord, madam,*'—

OLIVIA

How now! Art thou mad?

CLOWN

No, madam, I do but read madness: an your ladyship will have it as it ought to be, you must allow *Vox*.

OLIVIA

Prithee, read i' thy right wits.

CLOWN

So I do, madonna; but to read his right wits is to read thus: therefore perpend, my princess, and give ear.

OLIVIA

[*To Fabian*] Read it you, sirrah.

FABIAN

[*Reads*] *'By the Lord, madam, you wrong me, and the world shall know it: though you have put me into darkness and given your drunken cousin rule over me, yet have I the benefit of my senses as well as your ladyship. I have your own letter that induced me to the semblance I put on; with the which I doubt not but to do myself much right, or you much shame. Think of me as you please. I leave my duty a little unthought of and speak out of my injury.*

The Madly-used Malvolio.'

OLIVIA

Did he write this?

CLOWN

Ay, madam.

DUKE ORSINO

This savours not much of distraction.

OLIVIA

See him deliver'd, Fabian; bring him hither.

Exit Fabian

My lord so please you, these things furtherthought on,

To think me as well a sister as a wife,

One day shall crown the alliance on't, so please you,

Here at my house and at my proper cost.

DUKE ORSINO

Madam, I am most apt to embrace your offer.

[*To Viola*] Your master quits you; and for your

service done him,

So much against the mettle of your sex,

So far beneath your soft and tender breeding,

And since you call'd me master for so long,

Here is my hand: you shall from this time be

Your master's mistress.

OLIVIA

A sister! You are she.

Re-enter FABIAN, with MALVOLIO

DUKE ORSINO

Is this the madman?

OLIVIA

Ay, my lord, this same.

How now, Malvolio!

MALVOLIO

Madam, you have done me wrong,
Notorious wrong.

OLIVIA

Have I, Malvolio? No.

MALVOLIO

Lady, you have. Pray you, peruse that letter.
You must not now deny it is your hand:
Write from it, if you can, in hand or phrase;
Or say 'tis not your seal, nor your invention:
You can say none of this: well, grant it then
And tell me, in the modesty of honour,
Why you have given me such clear lights of favour,
Bade me come smiling and cross-garter'd to you,
To put on yellow stockings and to frown
Upon Sir Toby and the lighter people;
And, acting this in an obedient hope,
Why have you suffer'd me to be imprison'd,
Kept in a dark house, visited by the priest,
And made the most notorious geck and gull
That e'er invention play'd on? Tell me why.

OLIVIA

Alas, Malvolio, this is not my writing,
Though, I confess, much like the character

But out of question 'tis Maria's hand.
And now I do bethink me, it was she
First told me thou wast mad; then camest in smiling,
And in such forms which here were presupposed
Upon thee in the letter. Prithee, be content:
This practise hath most shrewdly pass'd upon thee;
But when we know the grounds and authors of it,
Thou shalt be both the plaintiff and the judge
Of thine own cause.

FABIAN

Good madam, hear me speak,
And let no quarrel nor no brawl to come
Taint the condition of this present hour,
Which I have wonder'd at. In hope it shall not,
Most freely I confess, myself and Toby
Set this device against Malvolio here,
Upon some stubborn and uncourteous parts
We had conceived against him: Maria writ
The letter at Sir Toby's great importance;
In recompense whereof he hath married her.
How with a sportful malice it was follow'd,
May rather pluck on laughter than revenge;
If that the injuries be justly weigh'd
That have on both sides pass'd.

OLIVIA

Alas, poor fool, how have they baffled thee!

CLOWN

Why, 'some are born great, some achieve greatness, and some have greatness thrown upon them.' I was one, sir, in this interlude; one Sir Topas, sir; but that's all one. 'By the Lord, fool, I am not mad.' But do you remember? 'Madam, why laugh you at such a barren rascal? An you smile not, he's gagged:' and thus the whirligig of time brings in his revenges.

MALVOLIO

I'll be revenged on the whole pack of you.

Exit

OLIVIA

He hath been most notoriously abused.

DUKE ORSINO

Pursue him and entreat him to a peace:
He hath not told us of the captain yet:
When that is known and golden time convents,
A solemn combination shall be made
Of our dear souls. Meantime, sweet sister,
We will not part from hence. Cesario, come;
For so you shall be, while you are a man;

But when in other habits you are seen,
Orsino's mistress and his fancy's queen.

Exeunt all, except Clown

CLOWN

[*Sings*] *When that I was and a little tiny boy,*
With hey, ho, the wind and the rain,
A foolish thing was but a toy,
For the rain it raineth every day.

But when I came to man's estate,
With hey, ho, & c.
'Gainst knaves and thieves men shut their gate,
For the rain, & c.

But when I came, alas! To wive,
With hey, ho, & c.
By swaggering could I never thrive,
For the rain, & c.

But when I came unto my beds,
With hey, ho, & c.
With toss-pots still had drunken heads,
For the rain, & c.

A great while ago the world begun,
With hey, ho, & c.
But that's all one, our play is done,
And we'll strive to please you every day.

Exit